Cameron looked down at his arm. He could see metal. Mechanical components exposed through tears in his skin. The emotionless O of the mouth of a gun barrel.

There was no pain.

There was no blood.

His head swam as he watched strange mechanisms snick neatly back into place like the blades on a Swiss Army knife. He felt sick. Maybe it was the smell of gunsmoke, but he didn't think so.

What had been done to him?

About the author

When not writing books, Ben Horton loves directing and acting in plays. His dream is to star in a big-budget Hollywood version of Monster Republic. He is a long-time fan of superhero, science fiction and action movies and lives and works in London. This is his debut novel.

MONSTER MR REPUBLIC

Ben Horton

illustrations by Christian Scheurer

CORGI BOOKS

MONSTER REPUBLIC
A CORGI BOOK 978 0 552 56057 3

Published in Great Britain by Corgi Books,
an imprint of Random House Children's Books
A Random House Group Company

This edition published 2010

1 3 5 7 9 10 8 6 4 2

The Random House Group Limited supports the Forest Stewardship
Council (FSC), the leading international forest certification organization.
All our titles that are printed on Greenpeace-approved FSC-certified paper
carry the FSC logo. Our paper procurement policy can be found at
www.rbooks.co.uk/environment.

Set in Century Old Style

Corgi Books are published by Random House Children's Books,
61–63 Uxbridge Road, London W5 5SA

www.kidsatrandomhouse.co.uk
www.rbooks.co.uk

Addresses for companies within The Random House Group Limited can be
found at: www.randomhouse.co.uk/offices.htm

THE RANDOM HOUSE GROUP Limited Reg. No. 954009

A CIP catalogue record for this book is available from the British Library.

Printed in the UK by CPI Bookmarque, Croydon, CR0 4TD.

prologue

Even though it was well past midnight when the phone call came, Dr Lazarus Fry answered it before the second ring.

'Hello.'

'Is that you, Fry?'

'Yes, it is.'

Dr Fry didn't need to ask who the other voice belonged to. Only one person knew the number for the special hotline from London.

'Is it true?'

Dr Fry suppressed the urge to sigh. Like most scientists, he despised guessing games.

'Is what true, Prime Minister?'

'What I've just heard about the Divinity Project. That you've been spending government money on some sort of animal experiments.' The Prime Minister's voice was brimming with anger. His hatred of animal cruelty was well known. 'One of your lab technicians claims that you've been doing something with dogs.'

Dr Fry's narrow mouth twitched angrily.

'Who has been telling you this?'

'Some chap called Quinn. He says what you're doing down there in Broad Harbour is unethical. Illegal even.'

'Prime Minister,' said Dr Fry smoothly, 'let me assure you that everything that goes on in this laboratory is entirely within the law.'

'And have you got anything to do with these reports from the Broad Harbour police about strange creatures in the storm drains?'

Dr Fry laughed. 'Like the alligators in the New York sewers? Rumour and fantasy, Prime Minister. There is nothing amiss in Broad Harbour.'

The Prime Minister's voice sharpened.

'I'm afraid I don't share your opinion on that. You are to suspend work on the Divinity Project at once. I'm going to arrange for a team of independent investigators to come down next month and check out what's happening. If they find any evidence of wrongdoing, you will have me to answer to. Good night.'

With a sharp click, the line went dead.

Dr Fry sat quite still for a moment. Then he reached for another phone.

'Hardiman? I think we need to put the special contingency plan into operation. Oh, and Hardiman – pay Jason Quinn a visit, would you? Someone's been telling tales to the Prime Minister.'

Replacing the handset, Dr Fry picked up his scalpel and looked down into a pair of wide, terrified eyes.

'Now, where were we . . . ?'

chapter one

the technology of the future

The school trip was a disaster waiting to happen. Cameron Reilly just had no idea how big.

'Race you!' he shouted as he leaped off the coach. The journey from school hadn't been a long one but Cameron hated being cooped up, even for a few minutes.

Stretching his long, athletic legs, he sprinted off across the car park. His best friend, Darren, gave chase, but he had no chance of catching up. Although he was only fourteen, Cameron was already school football captain and could run the 100 metres in 12.5 seconds. He skidded to a stop at a set of automatic doors. A few seconds later, Darren arrived, puffing and blowing. Cameron was barely out of breath.

'You're going to have to do better than that if you want to make the team this season!' Cameron grinned, his blue eyes twinkling.

Darren took a moment to recover his breath – then punched Cameron's arm. 'Yeah, well, not all of us are pretty-boy wingers,' he retorted.

Cameron laughed. 'Who are you calling "pretty-boy"?'

'Don't pretend you didn't see Jane Chapman making eyes at you on the coach. Reckon she fancies you, mate.'

'Well, she can't have him,' interrupted a third voice. 'He's mine!'

The boys turned to see a tall, long-haired figure standing watching them.

'Oh, hi, babe,' said Cameron, slipping his arm around her slender waist.

Everyone agreed that Marie Lyons was the fittest girl in their class, and Cameron counted himself the luckiest guy in the school to have her for his girlfriend. They'd only been going out for a few months, but that was long enough for him to know that she was funny and smart as well as pretty. She hadn't even complained when he was late for their second and third dates because football practice had overrun. Cameron couldn't think of many girls who were so chilled about stuff like that.

'Mr Reilly!'

The sneering voice could only belong to Mr Hackford, the science master; an oily little man with a ratty moustache who took pleasure in trying to make his pupils feel as small as he was. He was the worst kind of teacher – the sort who always make really sarcastic 'jokes' that nobody else finds funny.

'I thought I had made it clear that this is a physics field trip, not a biology lesson. So kindly take your greasy paws off Miss Lyons and join the queue.'

'Yes, sir,' said Cameron obediently, dropping Marie's hand as they slipped into the line of students stretching back from the entrance to an ugly concrete building marked VISITOR CENTRE. Just ahead of them, a burly, shaven-headed boy used Mr Hackford's temporary distraction as an opportunity to barge in at the front of the queue, shoving a small kid sprawling to the ground and sending his glasses flying.

Mr Hackford spun round. 'Now, now! Settle down there!'

Eyes brimming, the boy got to his feet, rubbing a bleeding knee. Cameron vaguely recognized him from his computer science class. Nigel something.

'What's going on?' snapped Hackford.

Nigel looked back at his attacker, who just grinned menacingly, revealing a set of crooked teeth.

'Nothing, sir.' Nigel sniffed. 'I just fell over.'

The boy obviously didn't want to cause trouble. That figured – people who told tales on Carl Monkton usually regretted it. He wasn't afraid to use his fists to dole out punishment, and he had a reputation as a dirty fighter.

'Monkton's such a jerk,' hissed Cameron to Marie. 'Someone should take him down a peg or two.'

'Yes, but not you. Remember what happened last time?'

A few weeks earlier, Cameron had come across Carl picking on another nerdy boy behind the gym block. They had been squaring up for a fight when one of the PE teachers turned up and put them all in detention. But that had only postponed the inevitable. Cameron and Carl had hated each other ever since their first day at Broad Harbour High School. Sooner or later there would be a scrap. They both knew it was only a matter of time.

Cameron's intervention did have one unexpected side effect, though. The nerd he rescued spent the next two weeks trailing around after Cameron, imagining that the whole business had somehow made them friends. Although he did nothing for

Cameron's street cred, he did provide a couple of useful hints on homework assignments.

'Anyway,' continued Marie, 'let's just stay out of trouble and try to have fun.'

'Yeah, right,' grumbled Cameron as the queue started shuffling in through the doorway. 'A school outing isn't really my idea of fun. It's going to take a *lot* to make this trip exciting . . .'

'Welcome to Broad Harbour Nuclear Power Plant. In the event of a reactor core failure, please make your way to the nearest exit.'

Cameron shook his head. The recorded voice sounded so chirpy it could have been advertising washing-up liquid rather than warning about nuclear meltdown.

'In the event of a reactor core failure,' muttered Marie, 'we'd probably all be dead.'

'Or worse.' Cameron chuckled. *'In the event of a reactor core failure,'* he continued in a pretty good imitation of the announcer's inanely cheery voice, *'please make your way into town and eat as many brains as you can, because you'll all be radioactive zombies.'*

Marie giggled. 'Come on.'

The Visitor Centre was filled with scale models of the power plant and computer animations of how a nuclear reaction worked, as well as a load of other boring-looking displays on huge boards. It was all part of a major exhibition on sustainable energy paid for by the Fry Foundation, Broad Harbour's biggest charity. It was called 'The Technology of the Future'. As far as Cameron could make out from a quick skim, that meant things like harnessing the waves and geothermal energy. And he suspected that it was no coincidence that 'The Technology of the Future' was also the title for the project they were supposed to be working on in science that term. No wonder Mr Hackford had been so excited about the trip. All around him, Cameron could see his classmates digging into their bags for pads and pens. Some of the swots had already filled more than a page of their notebooks.

Well, that suited Cameron fine. So long as someone was making plenty of notes he could borrow, that meant he could relax. Besides, as well as being drop-dead gorgeous, Marie was super bright, so she was probably taking in lots of facts even while they were laughing and joking around.

'Hey, look!' She pointed. Nearby, Mr Hackford was trying to explain the process of nuclear fission to a blank-faced Darren. 'Looks like someone needs rescuing . . .'

Marie led the way over. 'Sir? Mr Hackford?'

'Yes, Marie?'

'I thought this exhibition was about the future. Who gets excited about nuclear power any more?'

Cameron bit his lip and concentrated on keeping a straight face.

'I mean, it's not very safe, is it?' she continued. 'What about that place that blew up and created all those mutant sheep? Chernobyl.'

'That was many years ago. And it was in Ukraine. Nuclear power stations are much safer and much cleaner than they used to be.'

'Yes, but they can still explode, can't they?'

'Yes, Miss Lyons,' snapped Hackford. 'They can, and so can I. And you and Mr Reilly have already tested my patience quite sufficiently today. Do I make myself clear? Now, if you'll excuse me . . .'

The trio waited for Mr Hackford's retreating form to disappear behind a huge plasma screen before bursting into laughter.

'Thanks, guys,' said Darren.

Marie grinned. 'Saved you from death by boredom!'

Cameron loved Marie's wicked sense of humour. She'd already made the day's ordeal a lot easier to bear. He didn't mind science, even found some of it interesting – especially practical experiments – but it wasn't really his thing. He was much more into sports and activities. And his race with Darren in the car park was probably going to be the most activity he'd get today.

'Come on,' said Cameron. 'Let's go and look at the upper level.'

They walked over to the winding metal staircase that led to the high gallery. From the ground floor, it looked as if the upper level contained more of the same sort of exhibits.

A few students were already up there, and there seemed to be some sort of commotion. It was no surprise that the familiar figure of Carl Monkton was at the centre of it. He had pinned Nigel against the gallery railing and, as Cameron stared, he hoisted the smaller boy up by his lapels and leaned him backwards as if he was going to tip him over.

'Reckon you can fly, Smith?'

The kid whimpered and sobbed.

Cameron swore and glanced around. Mr Hackford was over on the other side of the exhibition, talking to a small group of students. There were no guides or other adults nearby. But somebody had to do something . . .

'Darren, go and get Hackford, quick. Marie, you stay here.'

As Darren ran off, Cameron grabbed hold of the banister and raced up the stairs. Behind him, he could hear Marie's feet clanging on the metal steps. He should have known she wouldn't stay behind. Marie hated bullies.

'OK, Carl,' said Cameron levelly as he

reached the gallery. 'Put him down. Here, on the upstairs level, if you don't mind.'

'All right, Mr Perfect,' said Carl, shooting Cameron an ugly look and shoving Nigel roughly aside. 'Come on then, Reilly. Want to have a go yourself?'

Cameron stood his ground, but refused to take the bait by getting any closer. 'Leave it, Carl. You're meant to be learning stuff today, not getting yourself a bloody nose.'

As soon as he'd said it, Cameron winced at the mistake. That was tantamount to a challenge, making it harder for Carl to back down.

Sure enough, Carl took a step forward, fists bunched.

'Come on then, Reilly,' he repeated. 'You want to learn something? I'll teach you.'

Cameron shrugged tightly. He couldn't see any way out of this now. Where the hell was Darren with Mr Hackford?

'Cameron,' warned Marie, from somewhere behind him.

Cameron raised his own fists, waiting for

Carl to make the first move. Ready for the first punch, and ready to give as good as he got.

The punch never came. The fight never happened. The day had bigger things in store for Carl and Cameron. Huge, life-changing things.

Starting with a massive explosion.

chapter two

rebooted

Cameron awoke with a jolt.

Bright light and fizzing shadows flashed across his vision, as if he was looking out from inside a television through a screen of static. Although his eyes refused to focus, he had the unnerving sensation of someone hovering closely over him. Too close.

His ears were struggling as well. He could hear a voice, but the words reached him as murmurs, like transmissions from a distant star, even though each one was delivered with a wash of hot, sour breath across his face.

Slowly – painfully slowly – the static resolved into shapes, the shapes into features, the features into a blurry face; one Cameron was vaguely sure he should recognize. But his brain felt as sluggish as his senses. He had a thumping headache, steady and rhythmic, like a pounding fist beating against his skull.

He forced a blink, but only one of his eyelids seemed to be working. The face above him smiled thinly.

'Well, that's something. Subject is responsive. At last.'

'Subject?' Cameron tried to repeat, but his voice sounded cracked and dry, as if he'd been crawling across a desert for a week.

Still, the word told him something. It sounded medical. Was he in hospital? Surely not. In hospital they called you a patient, not a 'subject'. But the man leaning over him seemed to be wearing a white coat. That meant he had to be a doctor, didn't it?

Yes, that was it! The man was a doctor. Cameron had seen him on the TV.

Perhaps he *was* in some strange kind of hospital, then. He certainly seemed to be lying down, but if he was in a bed, it could have done with being a lot more comfortable. It was hard and cold, and his head was resting on a solid, unyielding lump rather than a pillow.

Before he could croak out another question, a probing light pierced Cameron's eyes, blinding him.

'Hmm. Light filter has failed to engage.'

The words meant nothing to Cameron, but the speaker sounded disappointed.

'Pupils not equal, of course,' observed the voice, with a humourless chuckle. 'But reactive nonetheless.' The light vanished and the voice hardened. 'What do you remember?'

Cameron frowned. Was the doctor talking to *him*? He tried to force the blurred outline into a sharper image. With a super-human effort, he focused his eyes on the speaker.

Wispy white hair atop a high-domed head. A pale face, broad and bony at the cheeks, that narrowed to a pointed chin. Shrewd eyes magnified by thick lenses, fenced in with gleaming silver frames. He *did* know this man.

'Dr Fry?' said Cameron, his voice still rough.

Dr Lazarus Fry was something of a local celebrity. Massively rich, he lived in a gleaming modern house on the north side of Broad Harbour. The Fry Foundation, his personal charity, was always involved in some generous new project for the community – repairing a run-down school or building an orphanage. Cameron knew he should be in safe hands. But he didn't feel safe.

'Facial recognition,' remarked the doctor. 'And some evidence of intact memory.' He leaned closer, treating Cameron to an overly clear view of flaring nostrils. 'But *what* do you remember?' he repeated.

Cameron frowned again, thinking back. His memory was foggy, but faint images jostled together in his mind: a large building filled with children; a thick-set boy with his fists raised; bright, blossoming orange light.

'An explosion. We were . . . We were on a school trip.'

But where am I now?

Cameron tried to turn his head to get a better view of the room he was in, but it wouldn't budge a centimetre. They must have strapped his head in place. Had he broken his neck? Concentrating, Cameron tried to flex his arms and legs, but his limbs didn't respond. It was as if his brain had been disconnected from the rest of his body. Panic flooded him.

'Am I hurt?' he croaked.

As Cameron spoke, another jolt of pain shot through him. It was gone as quickly as it had arrived, but it left his nerves tingling and jittery, like a mega-bad case of pins and needles.

'Hmm,' said Dr Fry, standing up. To Cameron's hazy senses it seemed as if the man's face was floating away from him into the air.

Fry raised an instrument over Cameron's body – something that looked like a mobile phone or Nintendo DS – and inspected the screen. He pursed his bloodless lips and shook his head.

'W-w-what is it?' stammered Cameron. 'Am I going to die?'

The doctor ignored him, turning instead to address someone out of Cameron's field of vision. 'Barely acceptable. This will do for our first objective, but I think we can do much, much better. Store it and bring me the next subject.'

'Yes, Dr Fry,' said a gruff voice.

Cameron heard footsteps shuffle closer, felt a jab in his left shoulder. Cold poured into his arm, and the static started to buzz across his vision again, like a TV that had lost its signal.

Then the screen went dead.

Cameron woke again.

His head was still pounding and he was freezing – as though he'd woken up in a fridge. And instead of the fuzzy vision there was only darkness. He shivered.

A shadow flitted past him in the gloom.

Cameron jumped, his whole body jerking. But at the same instant that one part of his mind registered the shock, another part registered overwhelming relief. Whatever was wrong with him, he wasn't paralysed!

The shadow flicked by again, brushing softly against his shoulder. He flinched, trying to pull away. There was a rapid series of clicks, and suddenly Cameron found he could move his right arm.

That was when he twigged: he had been strapped down, his arms and legs securely fastened with metal restraints. The shadow was unfastening them.

'What . . . what's going on?'

'*Shhhh,*' hissed someone. 'Stay still.'

A girl's voice, soft and throaty. She hurried down towards his right leg and began to work on the strap there.

Whoever she was, Cameron wished that she had started with the one securing his head. The only view he had was of a darkened ceiling. But with his right hand free, he ought to be able to release his head himself.

Cameron lifted his arm. It felt heavy and clumsy, as though he'd been sleeping on it all night. His hand fumbled uselessly at the strap across his forehead, fingers searching for the buckle or clasp.

'What's going on?' he said. 'What's happened to me? Am I hurt? Am I in hospital or what?'

The shadow threw aside the strap on his right leg and was around to his left in a flash. 'Sorry, but we're going to have to save the questions for later. My name's Rora and I'm here to help you, and that's all you're going to get for now.' She tugged the leg restraint loose, then moved to the one on his left arm. 'We have to get out of here.'

Whoever this girl was, she didn't sound much like a nurse. But then this place didn't feel much like a hospital. Cameron swallowed hard. He didn't really want to consider the other possibilities.

He was getting nowhere with the strap at his head. His fingers might as well have been a bunch of sausages, they were so numb and useless. What was wrong with him? Why was nobody willing to tell him what was going on?

Neither the doctor nor this strange girl. And where were his mum and dad?

Cameron tried clenching and unclenching his fingers to get some feeling back into them, but they weren't co-operating. At last Rora undid the last of his straps and his head was free. Impatiently he sat up straight and looked around.

Dizziness swamped him. His head reeled as his vision snapped into crystal-clear focus. It was as if someone had switched on a bright light inside his head. The sudden sharpness was overwhelming. No matter how much he shook his head to try to get rid of it, it stayed stubbornly with him. What did it mean?

Cameron scanned the room, fighting the giddiness. The lights were out, but despite the darkness he could make out rows of beds and tables, all shrouded with white sheets. This, combined with the freezing temperature, reminded Cameron uncomfortably of a morgue. And all he had on was a loose-fitting hospital gown. Terrific.

'Come on,' said Rora, helping him – practically dragging him – to his feet.

Cameron staggered, his legs wobbling. He bumped against whatever it was he had been lying on, and turned round to look at it. The metal medical trolley trundled a short distance before coming to rest against one of the beds.

'This isn't right,' he insisted. 'They don't keep patients on trolleys. They don't keep them in the freezer unless they're . . .' He scrubbed that thought right away: clearly he wasn't dead. 'Well, unless they're not patients any more.'

'Never mind that,' said Rora. 'Can you walk?'

'Of course I can,' hissed Cameron, gritting his teeth as an agonizing flash of pins and needles raced up his legs. He took a tottering step, his whole body feeling wobbly. He tried to take another, but as he threw his left leg forward, he overbalanced, almost falling. Rora leaped forward to steady him. Cameron stiffened, pushing her away far less gently than he'd intended.

'Give me a minute,' he snapped.

With a low growl, Rora backed off. Regaining his balance, Cameron stared at her. Even with his strange, super-clear vision, he couldn't get a good view of the girl's face; it was shrouded under a hood, but he could see that her skin was dark. Although she didn't look hostile, there was something odd about her that he couldn't quite pin down. For the moment, though, he had bigger things to worry about.

Like walking.

Aiming for one of the nearer beds, Cameron took another step. His movements were leaden and awkward, but his legs didn't feel as if they were about to give out. They felt firm enough, just . . . different. As if he was learning to walk on a pair of iron stilts. The dizziness didn't make it any easier.

'Maybe this is what it's like to be drunk,' he muttered.

'Get used to it. Quickly. I'm going to check the coast is clear.'

Rora raced to the door, so light on her feet that Cameron barely heard her footsteps. It made him envious and even more impatient.

Gritting his teeth, he stepped forward. He was just out of practice, that was all. He'd probably been lying still for too long, and his legs had gone to sleep. Or maybe the doctor had given him a sedative and he just had to wait for the effects to wear off. If he could get the blood pumping, he would be as right as rain. At least as athletic as this Rora girl. Sports Day Champion again.

Stumbling a bit, but feeling more confident with every stride, Cameron covered the distance – step by step – to the bed. As he arrived, though, a fresh dizzy spell ambushed him. He thrust out an arm to steady himself on the edge of the bed.

His hand touched something soft through the sheet. Reaching down, Cameron took hold of the sheet and lifted it gingerly aside.

There, burned and tattered, lay a human arm – with no body attached.

Cameron let out a yell and staggered

backwards. He threw out a hand, flailing for something to hold onto, but instead his knuckles crashed into a nearby machine, sending a tray of equipment clattering to the floor.

But there was no time to worry about what he'd knocked over.

After a split-second of silence, alarms rang out loud enough to wake the dead.

chapter three

the hunt

Sirens blared in Cameron's ears as he ran. It was as if a noise had drilled its way into his head and now it was stuck, screaming for a way out. Rora raced down the corridor just ahead of him. She seemed to know where she was going. All Cameron could do was follow at a sort of stumbling sprint.

His head reeled. Wherever he was, he was seeing it for the first time – and it was all shooting by in fast-forward: white-tiled floors, coloured numbers on the walls, closed doors with windows offering glimpses into different laboratories. And no time to stop for a look.

Letters jumped out at him from a sign mounted on the wall: DIVINITY PROJECT – NO UNAUTHORIZED ENTRY.

What about unauthorized exits?

Cameron fired a glance over his shoulder, but couldn't hear any sounds of pursuit. Then again, he couldn't hear Rora's footfalls or even his own above the constant din. He barely heard her yell as she skidded to a stop at a corner, nearly crashing into her.

Two white-suited technicians barred their path, one of them wielding some sort of needle-gun.

'Back up!' Rora shouted, tugging him in the other direction. Now they were running again, back the way they'd come.

And something strange was happening. Somehow Cameron knew the alarms were screaming out as loud as ever, but they *seemed* to be getting quieter. As if his ears were filtering out the blare and tuning in to the more important sounds. Like the rapid beat of footsteps behind them – the technicians giving chase.

31

Rora sped on, leading them back towards the very room where they'd started. She ducked inside and pulled Cameron in after her.

'What are you doing?' he protested. 'This is a dead end. If they find us—'

Rora clapped a hand over his mouth as a pair of white suits flashed past the doorway and on down the corridor.

'Right,' whispered Rora breathlessly. 'Let's try that again.'

With a quick glance to ensure the technicians were continuing in the other direction, she led Cameron back out into the corridor and raced along, following their original escape route. 'Figured they'd never look in the lab we broke out of!' she explained.

Cameron nodded. That was smart, but it had been one heck of a gamble. If the technicians had seen them, they would both have been cornered in there.

But this wasn't the time to be thinking of 'ifs'. Too many of those lay ahead. And although Cameron was grateful for whatever was dimming the alarms and allowing him to pick out other sounds, it wasn't doing anything for his dizziness. Nor were the hundreds of questions reeling around inside his head.

There was only time to ask one as Rora skidded to a halt to heave open a heavy door.

'Where are we going?'

Before Rora could answer, a bloodcurdling howl – like the cry of some mad, starved animal – echoed through the building. Suddenly Cameron wished he could go back to hearing nothing but alarms.

Rora stared, terrified. 'My God,' she said. 'He's set the Bloodhounds on us.'

'Bloodhounds? What?'

'No time! Just run!'

She was through the door. Cameron had to grab it to stop it from swinging closed, then he was slipping after her and half charging, half tripping down a staircase. Rora had summoned an extra burst of speed from somewhere and was already way ahead of him. There was no catching up with her.

Cameron ground his teeth with frustration. What was wrong with him? He'd never been outrun by a girl . . .

Three flights below, Rora crashed through another pair of doors – and straight into trouble.

Cameron heard the girl cry out but, more than that, he just *knew*. It was as though every one of his instincts had kicked up a gear. Before he could even think, something inside him took over, and he was vaulting over the banister and out into space.

He'd never done *that* on Sports Day.

Dropping down half the height of the stairwell, watching the floor rushing up at him – Cameron braced himself for the landing, fully expecting to break his legs. Then he hit the ground.

He felt the shock of the impact vibrating up his calves, but there was no pain. What was more, he was poised in a sort of judo stance, ready for action. Cameron shook his head – he didn't even know judo. Something really *had* taken over.

He powered through the doors. What stood beyond was like nothing he'd ever seen.

The three figures seemed to be some hideous hybrid of man, machine and animal. Canine muzzles snarled out of human faces, fleshy lips peeling back from metallic jaws that dripped crimson-flecked drool.

Bloodhounds.

One of the growling beasts had pinned a choking Rora to the wall by the throat; her feet kicked uselessly a metre off the ground. The other pair eyed Cameron, snarling hungrily, their gleaming fangs bared and ready, like cybernetic werewolves defying him to make any kind of move.

Cameron sprang forward. It should have been hopeless – suicidal. He should have been scared out of his wits by the mere sight of these impossible creatures. And maybe, somewhere at the back of his mind, part of him was. But most of him just saw red. A furious, frenzied red in which his arms lashed out with a will of their own. Where he whirled to face one attacker and sent it reeling with a power-driven kick; flattened another with a tooth-crunching punch to the chin.

It was as if someone had stepped into Cameron's head and taken control of his body; as if he was a character in a computer game. Everything was in razor-sharp focus: the snarling, snapping jaws; the claws slashing in at him; his own arms shooting out to block the attacks. And yet somehow it all rushed by in a blur of continuous motion. It wasn't even like fighting by instinct; it was like fighting in a dream – or a nightmare.

Two of the Bloodhounds were already slumped unconscious on the floor, shaggy piles of fur and metal. The final one had dropped Rora and was now being driven relentlessly backwards by Cameron's swinging fists. Desperately he fought to regain control of them, but it was like swimming against the tide. His limbs seemed to have a mind of their own.

Sweeping the Bloodhound's feet from under it with a low, raking kick, Cameron felt his arm swing back to unleash a final punch. Mustering every ounce of concentration, he tried to hold the blow back. For an instant his arm wavered, hesitant.

And in that moment the Bloodhound struck.

Horrified, Cameron saw the monster leap forward. Saw it sink its steel teeth into his right forearm and the fangs tear his skin. He waited for the dream to end. For the burning pain, the gush of blood. But instead, he felt something revolving *inside* his arm, clicking into place like a key in a lock. Then there was a sharp bang – and suddenly Cameron was wide awake. Brought right back down to earth by the acrid smoke drifting up past his eyes.

The Bloodhound staggered away, whining and clutching at its belly, its doggy eyes screwed up in pain. Then it keeled over and collapsed in a heap.

Cameron looked down at his arm. He could see metal. Mechanical components exposed through tears in his skin. The emotionless O of the mouth of a gun barrel.

There was no pain.

There was no blood.

His head swam as he watched strange mechanisms snick neatly back into place like the blades on a Swiss Army knife. He felt sick. Maybe it was the smell of gunsmoke, but he didn't think so.

What had been done to him?

Then, like the precise components revolving in his arm, Cameron's memories fell neatly into place: the severed arm in the lab; his strange, disorienting night vision; the alarms he'd filtered out; that insane leap down the stairwell. And now this.

Suddenly he was aware of Rora watching him, massaging her throat.

'What's happened to me, Rora?'

She opened her mouth, but she appeared lost for words, or breath.

Cameron glanced around, his gaze falling on the reflective window of a nearby laboratory. Slowly he started walking towards it.

'Cameron, don't. Not yet.'

Rora's voice seemed to come from a long way behind him. Maybe he had filtered it out, like the alarms. She reached for him, but he shook her off.

Cameron fixed his eyes on the window. He stepped forward. And there, in the glass, he found his reflection waiting for him.

chapter four

monster

The face that stared back at Cameron was not his own.

He had thought the Bloodhounds gruesome enough. This face possessed no canine jaws, but that was the smallest of mercies. Scars, scabs and livid bruises stained the skin an ugly mess of colours – red, brown, blue, black, purple. The whole top right quarter of the face had no skin at all, just an expanse of dull, grey steel. The eye that gazed out from this metal plating looked more like a camera. Its cold, glassy lens stared back at him from alongside a living, human eye, daring Cameron to keep looking. Sending him the clear and brutal truth: *This is you.*

'No,' he whispered to the monster in the

glass. And he watched it shaking its hideous head. 'That's not me. *You're* not me.'

Almost acting of their own accord again, Cameron's fingers reached out to touch the window, as if testing to see if it was broken or warped. Or maybe to make certain that the glass was really there, that he wasn't looking at some grotesquely distorted projection.

No. The glass was real and smooth.

He brought his hand back towards the ragged, crudely stitched patchwork of flesh and metal that was his face. Maybe it was only a mask – something he could take off, somebody's sick joke. But his fingers hovered centimetres from his cheek, too terrified to touch.

Suddenly he was dragged away from the hideous reflection and became aware of Rora's firm grasp on his arm.

'This is no time to be admiring yourself.'

Turning to face her, Cameron got his first proper close-up look at Rora too. She was smaller than he had realized, tiny and lithe, with dark, elfin features. The darkness didn't come from her skin, though, but from the wash of deep auburn hair that seemed to be growing from her face and hands as well as her head.

Rora met his gaze challengingly.

'Don't think about what you saw in that reflection. Nobody looks their best when they've just woken up.'

Cameron's fists clenched. 'This isn't funny!'

'No, I know – it's anything but. You're just going to have to trust me. Because we're not out of the woods yet!'

Dazed and numbed, Cameron didn't resist as Rora grabbed his hand and yanked him back into a run. They raced down the corridor, through another pair of doors and into another stairwell. This time, she propelled Cameron ahead of her and he lurched down the steps, three or four at a time. She grabbed the banister and swung herself round each bend. They were at the bottom in a matter of seconds.

Above, Cameron could hear pursuers charging through the doors, followed by pounding footsteps coming down the stairs. Another unearthly howl sliced through the air, sending shivers down his spine.

Without looking back, Rora ushered Cameron into what looked like a basement passage. Bare cinder-block walls replaced the clinical white of upstairs, and low-hanging pipes and cables forced them to duck as they ran. Cameron didn't imagine there could be many ways to escape from a basement.

'What are we meant to do? Dig our way out?'

Ignoring him, Rora raced forward and swerved round a corner. Behind them, the thump-thump of footfalls. Cameron glanced back to see a fresh mob of Bloodhounds racing down the last few stairs, flashing their steel fangs. Spotting him, the monsters dropped onto all fours and loped hungrily towards him, their eager breaths and snarls sounding loud and dangerously close in the confines of the passage.

Cameron careered round the corner and found himself facing a massive metal door.

Just in the process of swinging ponderously open, it was a solid metre thick, like the door of a bank vault. Behind them, the Bloodhounds rounded the final corner, slavering heads down as they pounded along, their four limbs eating up the last few precious metres between them and their prey.

'Down here!' howled one triumphantly. 'Waste disposal!'

Rora was already on the other side of the door, tapping frantically at a keypad on the wall. Cameron leaped through to join her as the door started swinging shut.

But it wasn't going to be fast enough. The Bloodhounds were too close.

Seizing the large wheel in the centre of the door, Cameron braced his feet against the frame. The massive door was so huge that his strength couldn't possibly speed it up, but he had to try. Taking a deep breath, he heaved.

To his surprise, pulling the massive metal barrier inwards was no more difficult than closing his bedroom door. With a screech of protest, the door swung towards him, fast. Staggering backwards, Cameron just had time to catch a last glimpse of the Bloodhounds, rocketing along the passage like fanged missiles, before the door slammed shut.

Cameron found himself sprawled on his back, with Rora standing over him, open-mouthed.

'Enhanced strength,' she breathed, helping him to his feet. 'You're quite something.'

Feeling uncomfortable under Rora's appraising gaze, Cameron took a swift look around. They were standing on a metal walkway, above a large cellar filled with grubby pipes and a dormant generator in the far corner. Below them, a conveyor belt ran into the mouth of a huge machine, receding into darkness like a tunnel. There were no doors anywhere.

Dead end.

Rora didn't seem bothered, however. 'Lucky for us Professor Freakenstein likes to dispose of his rubbish in private,' she said briskly. 'So the Bloodhounds can't open the door without the override code – but that won't hold them for long.'

On cue, there was an almighty bang, like a battering ram slamming against the door. The walls shook. Incredibly, a dent bulged out on the inside. It was rapidly followed by another hefty slam – and another. It was unbelievable, but it looked as if the monsters would have the door off its hinges soon.

'Maybe I could take them,' said Cameron doubtfully. He had no desire to experience another fight like the last one, but it didn't seem as if the Bloodhounds were going to give him a choice in the matter.

'Reinforcements will be coming. Who d'you think it was shouting to? It's time to go.'

'Go where? In case you hadn't noticed, we're trapped in here – unless you're suggesting . . .'

Rora nodded down towards the gaping mouth of the waste disposal machine, framed with gigantic metal teeth. Rotten air wafted out from the hidden depths like bad breath.

'No,' said Cameron. 'No way.'

Rora made a regretful face. 'Sorry.'

'For what?'

'This.'

She gave Cameron a hefty shove, catching him off balance and pitching him over the catwalk railing and down . . .

Cameron landed on his feet – but also on the conveyor belt, where Rora had wanted him. She leaped off the catwalk and landed gracefully beside him.

'Come on!' she shouted. 'What're you standing around for?'

Cameron peered into the ghastly machine, casting wary glances at the succession of mashers and serrated teeth lining the interior, with further pile drivers and crushing devices beyond, receding into darkness. Darren had once dared him to stick his head into the mouth of one of the huge dinosaur skeletons in Broad Harbour Museum, but Cameron had refused. The great jaws might have looked still and dead, but he hadn't been able to shake off the thought that they might snap unexpectedly shut . . .

'I can't,' he said quietly.

'Then you're dead,' replied Rora.

Above them there was a sudden tremendous crash, and Cameron knew that the Bloodhounds had broken through the door. He glanced up. Half a dozen of the cybernetic canines barrelled in and fanned out menacingly on the walkway.

There was no way they could stand and fight. That realization, more than Rora's urging, provoked Cameron into action.

'Come on, then!' He dashed headlong into the darkness, Rora keeping pace beside him.

Gruff animal shouts echoed after them.

'They went into the machine!' roared one of their pursuers.

Another gave a throaty laugh. 'Fire it up, then!'

Cameron shot a panicked look at Rora as the whine of heavy machinery started up all around them, like some industrial dragon waking. Hisses of steam and the groan of hydraulics added to the terrifying impression.

Ahead of them, a set of enormous steel jaws ground themselves slowly together, then slid apart, before clanging together again.

'The longer we take, the harder it's going to get!' Rora snapped.

She was right – the machine's rhythm was already picking up speed. Pausing for a second, Rora leaped forward, just as the metal teeth parted once more.

BAM!

They closed again behind her. Cameron took a deep breath.

BAM! They hit again, then slid apart. Cameron dived forward. *BAM!*

He was through, and rolling onto his feet to face the next set of crushers.

Cameron winced: it was just like one of those video games where you had to time your jumps to avoid some death-trap. He'd been OK on games like that, but sometimes it took him two or three tries to get through.

This time, though, he didn't have any lives to spare.

Rora sprang. *BAM!* Cameron waited. *BAM!*

Cameron dived through. *BAM!*

Then the next.

BAM! Rora. *BAM!* Wait. *BAM!* Cameron. *BAM!*

The final obstacle looked less fearsome: a pair of metal blocks, designed to pound up the rubbish after the jaws had cut it into manageable portions. But this time Rora was hesitating, and Cameron could see why. The crushers were already going too fast.

BAM! BAM! BAM! The metal fists slammed together, practically no time at all between blows. *BAM! BAM! BAM!*

They had to keep taking paces backwards just to stand still, as the conveyor tried to advance them towards the crushers.

Behind them, with the sharp-toothed jaws, it was the same story: *BAM! BAM! BAM!*

Trapped.

Rora looked at Cameron, desperation in her eyes. She was supposed to be the one leading him out of here, but this hadn't been part of the plan.

Cameron's mind raced, faster and faster,

like the machine. The pounding filled his head, reminding him of the Bloodhounds and the way they had smashed down the huge door. The one he had closed so easily.

He glanced at his arms. If they really *were* that strong, then maybe ...

There was only one way to put it to the test. Without a word, Cameron dived forward past Rora. Throwing wide his arms, palms outwards, he wedged himself between the closing blocks of steel. He heard Rora cry out, a millisecond too late.

But his own timing was spot on. Unbelievably, he was between the crushers, holding them apart. His arms strained. He could hear the waste disposal machine groaning in protest, while motors somewhere inside his body whined in reply as the fearsome metal fists pressed against him.

Cameron groaned. The blocks were still closing, centimetre by centimetre, as though the machine was determined to crush his bones to powder. He could feel his arms beginning to give way, and his heart sank.

Maybe he had overestimated his new strength after all.

Roaring, he pushed harder.

Strength Cameron never dreamed he had pumped through his veins, while sweat streamed out of every pore.

'Go! Go!' he shouted.

Rora's lithe form flipped past him. She was through!

Cameron swore. The groans of the machine were rising in pitch and he listened in mounting desperation. He hadn't thought this through properly. Yes, he had bought Rora enough time to get through, but now he was trapped, holding the crushers apart. As soon as he let go, the machine would smash him to a pulp.

'Jump for it!' yelled Rora above the shriek of machinery. 'It's your only chance.'

Sensing his muscle power – or his will-power – threatening to give out, Cameron fixed his gaze straight ahead. Taking one last lungful of breath, he tensed his legs, ready to spring.

Rora was right. It was his only chance.

Throwing his all into one final shove, he jumped.

BAM!

chapter five

reject

The jaws of the crusher slammed shut, missing Cameron by millimetres, chomping empty air behind him.

But there was no time to celebrate. Out of control, he knocked Rora flying, and suddenly they were both tumbling off the end of the conveyor belt, into a broad, steep-sided funnel.

Cameron hit the smooth side of the funnel, slick with oil and slime, and started slipping, sliding right past Rora. Looking down, he saw a dark chute at the bottom waiting to swallow them both.

'Bend your knees when you land!' Rora yelled.

'What?' Cameron bellowed, but he had run out of funnel and was already freefalling into darkness.

For the second time that day, instinct – instinct Cameron never knew he had – took over. Spinning cat-like in mid-air – with a flexibility he hadn't realized he possessed – he somehow turned himself upright, just in time to hit the ground. With a messy wet splash he found himself crouching in a fast-flowing stream of shallow water.

With the same suddenness as in the 'morgue', Cameron's sight immediately switched to night vision, drinking in every available drop of light. It might be in a slightly grainy monochrome, but he could see. The change was just as disorienting as before – and there wasn't even a great deal to look at: a circular tunnel stretching off in either direction, dank brick walls, and mucky water flowing around his shins. Water that presumably carried off most of the ground-up rubbish from the chute.

As his eyes adjusted, Cameron's nose also

came under immediate assault. Wherever he was, it stank. And now, on top of his dizziness, he was feeling sick. At least it was easy to tell where this strange girl had landed him: right in the—

Rora splashed down next to him.

She didn't give Cameron a chance to complain. She just leaped up, grabbed his hand and towed him after her. He stumbled, found his footing, and let her drag him forward while his mind struggled to catch up. He had a horrible suspicion that all the changes he had discovered in himself back in the lab were just the beginning. He dreaded to think what else might have been done to him.

They ran silently for five minutes, Cameron's ears picking up no sound of pursuit. A T-junction loomed ahead. Surely they could afford a pause for some much-needed answers?

Cameron slackened his pace, but Rora gave his arm a sudden tug, urging a fresh burst of speed.

'Hey!' He snatched his arm free and stopped in his tracks.

Rora rounded on him. 'Shout a bit louder, why don't you? Make it easier for them! Give them a minute and they'll realize we made it through the waste disposal machine. Then they'll be down here after us for sure!'

Cameron threw up his arms. 'So? Maybe I *want* to be found!'

'Take it from me, you *don't*.'

'Why? Why should I take anything from you? Who *are* you? I don't know you. I'm only in trouble because you dragged me out of there and shoved me in a rubbish crusher! I haven't had time to stop and think. Those alarms were doing my head in and now my eyes . . .' He waved a hand in front of his face. 'I don't know *what's* going on with them, but they're giving me a headache too!'

'Heightened senses,' said Rora impatiently, looking up and down the tunnel. 'You'll get used to it. Learn to control it all.'

Cameron made a face. 'What if I don't want to?'

'Want's got nothing to do with it. It's what you are.'

'No way. This isn't who I am. This is what I woke up as, after the accident.'

'That was no accident,' muttered Rora cryptically. 'Come on. Freedom beckons. But if we don't get moving, it's not going to be an option.'

As though to back her up, shouts and splashing footsteps suddenly sounded in the distance. A searching torch beam probed the gloom. Cameron flinched at the intrusion of bright light.

He whirled round to face Rora and shook his head. 'No. I don't have to run. They're only chasing us because they want me back. You can get out, but I'm going back there – where I can get some answers. Where someone can fix this.'

Rora spat. 'Don't you get it? You *are* fixed! This what you are now. But we can help you.'

'Who can? Where are you taking me?'

'Somewhere safe. Somewhere for people

58

like us. Rejects. We call it the Monster Republic. It's—'

'A place monsters can hang out?' scoffed Cameron. 'Well, that's the problem. I'm not a monster.'

'That's just it – you *are*! We all are!' She thrust out an arm, pointing back the way they'd come. 'You go back there and you're on your own! What's more you'll probably be dead. Dismantled.'

Cameron growled and spun away. His head was clearer now. He didn't trust this freaky girl, and he certainly didn't trust Dr Fry and his doggy friends. He needed time to think. Turning away from Rora and the torch beams, he stomped off through the mucky water.

'So where do you think you're going now?'

'Home!'

'You idiot! You don't have one any more!'

Cameron broke into a jog. His legs felt more under his control now. Behind him, he thought he heard Rora running off in the opposite direction. Good. He might not trust her, but he didn't want her to get caught by those Bloodhounds.

He jogged along the passage and soon came to another junction, where a ladder ascended into a narrow shaft above his head. Hesitating for a moment, he thought he could just make out a set of footsteps splashing their way after him. Grabbing the bottom rung of the ladder, Cameron began climbing.

Above, the surface and fresh air awaited him. And, hopefully, familiar ground.

Cameron cautiously lifted up the manhole cover and peered out. It was night and there didn't seem to be anybody about, both of which suited him fine.

He quickly clambered off the ladder and ducked into the shadows of a high wall to survey his surroundings: a tall block of flats and a short row of shops, all with blinds or metal shutters drawn down over their windows. For a moment Cameron didn't recognize the street; then he remembered – it was part of the housing estate out by the leisure centre where he came to go swimming with Marie.

Marie!

The memory of her hit Cameron like a bucket of cold water, and he felt instantly guilty for not thinking about her sooner. How could he have forgotten? What if she had been hurt in the explosion? What if she was dead?

It was Rora's fault, dragging him around, not giving him a moment to think, even about clothes: he was still wrapped in a now filthy hospital-type gown. He had to find something to wear, but most of all he had to find out if Marie was OK.

Cameron started walking, keeping close to garden walls, cutting through back streets and finding shadows wherever he could, moving faster wherever lamp-posts cast most light. He wished he could just call Marie, but he didn't have his phone or any money to use a callbox. And, he realized, he didn't even know Marie's number off by heart. He would just have to wait until he got home and through the ordeal of meeting his family. The thought of letting them see him – and what had been done to him – filled him with dread.

The journey took a dark and lonely hour, interrupted only by the passage of a car or the footsteps of pedestrians. People with some reason to be out, despite the lateness. People to be avoided.

Every time he heard an engine or sensed a set of headlights sweeping his way, Cameron dived over a garden hedge or ducked into a shadowed porch until they'd passed. Even though he had done nothing wrong, he felt like a criminal on the run.

Finally he turned the corner into his own street. He quickened his pace, opened the gate and walked up the path, just wanting to get inside his house, to stop running. He stopped at the front door and swore softly to himself.

His keys, along with his wallet, his phone and anything else he had been carrying at the time of the accident, were presumably stored somewhere at the lab he had just escaped from.

For a moment Cameron stared at the doorbell. Just one gentle press would bring his mum and dad to the door. They would call the police, get something done about Dr Fry, and talk about finding him, Cameron, some help. Maybe over a nice, normal cup of tea.

But he couldn't bring himself to do it. He had to break the news to his family in the right way. He didn't know exactly what that was, but ringing the doorbell at three in the morning definitely wasn't it.

Maybe he should get inside and wait for them to wake up? Cameron pondered the idea. If nothing else, it would put the moment off for a few more hours.

'Yeah,' he murmured to himself. 'That's it.'

There was still the question of how to get in, though.

Cameron took a deep breath and crept along the side of the house. As he rounded the corner, his heart jumped into his mouth. There was somebody in the garden! Waiting, silhouetted against the night sky. At first he thought it must be a Bloodhound. Then he realized. It wasn't a person at all, but a collection of clothes hanging from the washing line.

Odd. It wasn't like his mum to leave washing out overnight. And the rubbish hadn't been taken out either. Three full bin bags had been carelessly dropped by the back gate, rubbish spilling out of them.

No, not rubbish – clothes. In fact, weren't those his favourite jeans?

Dropping to his knees, Cameron took a closer look. He was right – the jeans were his, as was the jumper and all the clothes underneath.

'What are they doing out here?' he whispered to himself. His mum was always taking old clothes to the charity shop. But she didn't normally take his things without asking. Something wasn't right.

Pulling on some clothes, Cameron bunched up a T-shirt in his fist and tiptoed up to the back door. There was a tinkle of glass on the kitchen floor as he broke the window, but even to his super-sensitive ears, it didn't sound too loud. Reaching in, he worked the latch and slipped through the door.

Technically, he was home.

The house was deathly quiet and Cameron stood there for a long minute, just getting over the feeling of being an intruder. The kitchen looked just like it always did, neat and tidy, so Cameron made his way into the hall. It too looked normal: the row of coats behind the front door; the antique chair that his dad had bought at an auction; the cards on the old table.

Cards? Cameron frowned. It wasn't anyone's birthday. So why were there so many cards? Dozens of them. He crossed over to the table and picked one up. It had a picture of white lilies on the front, and words in loopy, hard-to-read writing:

With deepest sorrow for your loss.

Someone had died. Cameron's heart skipped a beat. Could it be his gran? She lived in Australia but she must have heard about his accident by now. She was old, well into her eighties. What if the shock had been enough to kill her?

'Please, not you,' he muttered, opening the card. He recognized his gran's handwriting at once. So it wasn't her who had died. Then who?

Cameron scanned the brief note inside.

Dear Keith, Laura and Shannon
I cannot tell you how sorry I am that I
can't be with you at this sad time.
Cameron was such a lovely, bright boy
with his whole life ahead of him. I will
miss him so much.
Love to you all,
Gran

Cameron staggered, his mind whirling. He thumped heavily into the table, knocking a spray of cards to the floor like confetti. Words leaped up at him: *With sympathy . . . Thinking of you . . . Sad to hear of your bereavement . . .*

Realization hit him like a speeding train.

His family thought he was dead.

That was why his mum had packed up all his clothes, and why she had forgotten to bring the washing inside. Somehow – *somehow* – they thought that he had been killed in the accident at the power plant. How was he going to explain . . . ?

'Who's there?'

A girl's voice. His sister's voice.

Startled, Cameron turned to see her poised nervously on the stairs. She hadn't changed – except for the dread in her eyes. It took him a second to recover his breath.

'Hi, Shan. It's me, Camer—'

'Shannon! Get back to your room!'

Dad's voice rang out down the stairs, making Cameron jump. Then his father was rushing after it, pushing past Shannon and ushering her back up behind him.

'Keith? What's going on?' Cameron could see his mum at the top of the stairs. 'Oh, my God! What is *that*?' She burst into tears, clasping a hand over her mouth.

'Stay where you are! I'll handle this!'

'Dad,' Cameron tried to say, but his voice was no more than a squeak. The look in his dad's eyes was every bit as frightening as the reflection he had seen in the lab window.

'Get out! Get out of our house this second!' Dad was shaking and, Cameron realized, so was he. 'My wife is calling the police right now!'

Nodding, Cameron's mum disappeared quickly from view.

Cameron called after her. 'Mum!'

'What's your problem? You're in the wrong house! You come near my family, I'll give you a bloody good hiding!'

Cameron moved forward. 'No, listen, it's me—'

He had barely taken a step before his dad rushed down at him. 'That's it!' he yelled. 'Get out!'

'Dad!' cried Shannon, her voice trembling. 'Be careful!'

And now his dad had hold of Cameron,

trying to force him away from the stairs. Cameron could still hear his mum crying, even as she spoke to someone on the phone. Crying himself, hurting inside, Cameron struggled to fend off his dad.

He tried to hold back, but this just seemed to provoke his dad into getting rougher and rougher. He shoved Cameron against the wall, turning over the hall table, scattering keys and mail, and raised a clenched fist. Cameron threw up an arm to parry the blow, then he shoved his father away – just trying to push him off and put some space between them. Space so he could talk, so he could explain.

But he had forgotten how strong he was now. Flying backwards, his dad lost his footing and Cameron heard a hefty thump as his head hit the stairs. Dad let out a pained groan and slumped to the floor, dazed.

Horrified, Cameron stared for a moment. Then he saw his sister staring back at him. Her eyes were filled with disgust and fear, and all the hateful emotions that cut deepest.

Head and heart reeling, Cameron turned

and ran for the door, doing his best to shut out the sound of his sister's screams and his Dad shouting, 'Yeah! You'd better run, whoever you are! Freak!'

Smashing through the front door as if it were paper, Cameron staggered out into the fresh night air. As he darted down the path, he was aware of lights coming on in nearby houses and neighbours emerging from their doors, drawn by the sounds of the fight.

Familiar faces. Surely someone would recognize him?

'Mrs Chatto,' Cameron shouted. 'It's me!' But their next-door neighbour only screamed as he lurched towards her, and rushed back inside her home.

Panic-stricken, he vaulted the gate and froze, looking left and right. Where should he go?

With a sick feeling, he realized it didn't matter. Left was as good as right. Rora had spoken the truth. He *didn't* have a home. He *was* a monster. And he *did* have to run – from the lab, from his family, from whatever he had become.

But *where*?

Quicker than he could make up his mind, at one end of the street a white van roared into view. It had no siren, but it cast flickering blue light everywhere, bringing more people to their doorways or out onto their front paths.

From the porch of the house opposite, Mrs Wyndham, who had been Cameron's babysitter for five years, called out, pointing: 'Police! There! There it is! Get it!'

The van pulled to a stop some metres away. The passenger door was thrown open and a man leaped out. But it wasn't the police. It was the all-too-familiar figure of Dr Lazarus Fry. His gaze fixed immediately on Cameron.

Dr Fry smiled, calmly and evenly. 'It's all right,' he said in a slow, firm voice, as if he was talking to a frightened animal. 'Everything will be all right.'

He glanced briefly around at the growing

crowd of muttering onlookers. Then he smiled at Cameron again, almost paternally. 'You're lost, you're frightened and I understand that. But if you just come with me, we'll get you all the help you need.'

The blare of a horn echoed from the opposite end of the street. Dr Fry's smile faded as Cameron turned to see a small figure racing up on a motor scooter.

Rora.

She braked some distance away, but kept the motor running. 'Cameron!' she yelled. 'You can't trust him! You belong with us! Come with me!'

Cameron was torn, his mind awash with confusion. Could he trust Rora? Yes, she'd broken him out of the lab, but he knew nothing about her.

On the other hand, there was Dr Fry. Perhaps the only man in the world who truly knew what Cameron was. Perhaps it would be best to go back to the lab. Back to where his new self had been 'born'.

But . . . Cameron couldn't shake off the

memory of the clinical way in which Fry had assessed him when he had woken up in the lab – or the cold, refrigerated room in which he had been stored like a slab of meat.

'Get it then! Take it away!'

From every direction, voices were jeering. The mood of the crowd was turning ugly. A bottle smashed at his feet, and above all the shouts Cameron heard the wail of approaching sirens. Finally the real police were on their way.

'Come along now,' said Fry, beckoning with an outstretched hand.

'Cameron! Come on!' yelled Rora. 'We have to go!'

The sirens were getting closer, fast. A stone whizzed past Cameron's ear.

He made his choice.

Ducking under a growing hail of missiles from the crowd, he sprinted over to the scooter and leaped onto the back. On either side, angry people shook their fists, but Cameron, holding on tight as Rora turned in a tight circle and accelerated away, didn't notice. He was staring over his shoulder, hoping for one last glimpse of home.

Instead, all he got was a view of Lazarus Fry, staring silently after him.

chapter six

the fox and the hounds

Rora drove them a few miles down lanes and back streets and into a small park. Cameron recognized it at once. He used to come here skateboarding because the hump-backed bridge was one of the few places in town that was good for stunts.

Stunts that paled into insignificance next to the speed at which Rora was steering the scooter through the winding paths. Still, even if they did end up wrapped around a tree, Cameron supposed he stood a far better chance of survival now than he would have done before Dr Fry had gone to work on him. He smiled bitterly. Watching superhero movies, he'd often thought how cool it might be to possess some of their powers. Now he did, but if he'd known that the price was to be rebuilt as a hideous mutant, he would have passed on the whole deal.

Rora brought the scooter skidding to a halt near a bench in a remote corner of the park.

'We should be OK here for a bit.'

Cameron climbed off and took a deep breath of night air, hoping it might cool his temper. It didn't.

'OK,' he said, rounding on Rora. 'So you've rescued me again. Now maybe you can tell me what's going on.'

'All right.'

Cameron looked up, surprised at her sudden willingness.

'Go on, then. I'm listening. My bionic ears could probably hear you from the other side of the park.'

Rora gave a sharp bark of laughter. She hopped up onto the bench and sat down on the back of it, feet planted on the seat.

'Right. This is going to sound incredible to

you, but you have to promise to hear me out.'

Cameron nodded slowly.

'OK, then,' began Rora. 'Dr Fry is working on something called the Divinity Project. The lab is his production line.'

'Production line for what?'

Rora took a deep breath. 'An army. The Divinity Project is a top secret government operation to design and build the next generation of soldiers.'

Cameron wasn't buying it. 'Well, if it's so top secret, how come *you* know about it?'

Rora's dark eyes fixed on Cameron.

'I was there.'

Cameron swallowed. 'At the lab?'

'How do you think I knew my way around?'

'What happened?'

Rora chewed a fingernail nervously. 'I was homeless when Dr Fry "saved" me.'

'Why were you homeless?'

'That doesn't matter to you. Didn't matter to my family. The important thing is, Dr Fry saved me – but only for himself. For his twisted experiments, anyway.'

'Experiments?' Cameron almost laughed – Rora made Fry sound like some mad professor. Then he remembered the fear and confusion of waking up on the trolley, and the laugh died in his throat.

He looked Rora up and down, but couldn't see any obvious mechanical additions.

'Well, they did a better job on the cosmetics with you than they did with me.'

'We're not the same,' replied Rora. 'I was an early project. You're a different product altogether.'

'So when were you there?'

'A couple of years ago.' Rora sounded impatient to get on with her story. 'The point is, the Fry Foundation picked me up off the streets. I thought I was headed for some care home or something. Instead, I ended up in a lab with a bunch of other street kids. He'd collected them from all over, apparently. As subjects.'

'*Subjects*,' echoed Cameron, recalling Fry's chillingly emotionless use of the word.

'Yeah, subjects. Fry was trying to blend

human genetics with animals, to create hybrid soldiers with cybernetic enhancements, like the Bloodhounds. But anyone who didn't come up to his exacting standards – well, you've seen the waste disposal system first hand.'

Cameron nodded, shuddering. 'Up close and personal.'

'And back in the early days, most of Fry's subjects *did* have some kind of weakness, and that just wasn't good enough for the doctor. Take me,' Rora continued. 'I'm quick. Brilliant reflexes, light on my feet – but I'm only good for short bursts. Stamina, I don't have.'

'So, wait – you were one of Fry's failures?'

'A Reject. Yeah.' Rora's voice held a strange blend of pride and bitterness. 'A few of us got wise to what happened to those who didn't make the grade, so we broke out. Some of us died in the attempt, but better to go out fighting for freedom than dumped in the crusher, yeah?'

'I guess,' grunted Cameron. There didn't seem to be any other answer.

'Anyway, those of us who escaped, we

banded together. The government didn't look after us, so we've created our own. We call it the Monster Republic. We don't have a home, but we had to at least give ourselves some kind of name. Makes us feel like we're part of something. Something that matters.'

Rora looked at Cameron seriously. He suspected she could see in his eyes the hard time he was having coming to terms with her fantastic story. Well, in the one eye that showed any human expression at all.

'Now we live in hiding,' she went on. 'Moving from place to place in the town, or under it. And for the last couple of years we've been doing what we can to strike back at Fry, trying to mess up his plans and make dents in this saintly reputation he's managed to build up for himself. You remember all those power cuts last winter?'

Cameron nodded.

'That was us. We were trying to interfere with a new load of experiments Fry was doing. We hoped the authorities might start investigating, but they didn't. Or if they did,

Fry managed to buy them off.' Rora's voice was low and bitter.

'We also watch the lab, looking out for other Rejects who manage to escape.' She stared hard at Cameron again. 'This was the first time we've broken back into the building though.'

Cameron shook his head. 'But why? Why now and why me?'

Rora sighed. 'This is where it gets complicated. About a month ago, our mole inside the lab, Jason, managed to make contact with the Prime Minister and tell him the truth about what the Divinity Project was doing. He was furious. Told Fry to suspend the project pending an investigation.'

'I'm not surprised,' said Cameron.

'Yeah, but Fry didn't suspend it,' replied Rora. 'He stepped it up. First, the day after he spoke to the Prime Minister, Jason vanished. Then, two days later, Fry collected a whole new bunch of subjects.'

'How?'

Rora bit her lip. 'He planted a bomb at Broad Harbour power plant.'

'Whoa, whoa, whoa!' Cameron raised his hands. This girl was getting way ahead of him. 'You're saying *Fry* caused the explosion? *Deliberately?*'

'Think about it: all the injured victims were taken to Fry's private clinic instead of the hospital. Right after the "accident", Fry made this big public announcement about how he was going to pay for special treatment, and make sure all those kids were given the best care possible. But surprise, surprise: so far none of them have managed to recover. Meanwhile – and this isn't public knowledge, of course – all the bodies of the dead kids were secretly transferred from the city morgue to the lab.'

'Wait,' repeated Cameron. 'When did you say this was?'

'Twenty-seven days ago.'

'Twenty-seven? I've been out of it for nearly a *month?*'

'I'm afraid so. I know that'll come as a shock.'

That was putting it mildly. Cameron shook

his head. A month had never sounded so long before.

'If you don't believe me, take a look at yourself,' said Rora. 'Fry didn't do all that work on you overnight.'

Cameron stared down at his right arm, where gears and pistons were still visible through the teeth-marks the Bloodhound had left in his artificial skin. What Rora was saying sounded impossible, but it did make a terrible, twisted sort of sense.

Rora pressed on relentlessly, hatred burning in her eyes like dark flame. 'Then, a couple of weeks ago, we found out more. Before he disappeared, Jason managed to plant a remote microphone in the lab. From a couple of conversations we overheard, we learned that Fry was using the bodies he'd harvested from the accident to build new human–machine hybrids more powerful than anything he'd achieved before. That was when we realized what he was up to.'

'What?'

'He was going to use them to destroy the

Monster Republic.'

'But why?' Cameron's head was spinning. He couldn't make sense of any of this.

Rora shrugged. 'We're a danger to him – the living proof of his botched experiments. If the Prime Minister's investigators found out about us, he would be finished.'

'So why don't you go to the police?'

'Yeah, right,' snapped Rora. 'Everyone in this town thinks Fry is their guardian angel. Who's going to believe a bunch of freaky-looking kids? We'd end up being stoned to death by an angry mob, or banged up in another lab, with another bunch of scientists running tests twenty-four/seven. No thanks.'

Cameron felt stupid for having even suggested it. He'd just experienced at first hand how 'normal' people had reacted to seeing him.

'Besides,' muttered Rora, 'we had a better plan. The first hybrid off this new production line was you. But it seems that you were only partially successful.'

Cameron remembered Fry leaning over

him, delivering his verdict: *Barely acceptable.* He'd never had anything nearly as damning as that in his school reports.

'Whatever the reason, Fry deactivated you while he built a second prototype,' Rora continued. 'But he didn't throw you away. That meant that sooner or later he was bound to break you out of storage and work on you some more – but we saw our chance.'

Rora was growing more animated now. 'From what we heard through Jason's mic, we knew that you hadn't been fully programmed when they shut you down. Not conditioned to obey Fry without question like the Bloodhounds are. So we figured that if we could spring you from the lab and get you on *our* side, we'd stand a chance of fighting back, whatever Fry had to throw against us. So that's why I came to find you, and that's why you're here.'

'No,' said Cameron, shaking his head as if he could dislodge the words that Rora had spoken. He refused to believe it. 'Cyborgs? Animal-human hybrids? A nutty professor working for the government blowing up a nuclear power station to create an army of mutants? This is science fiction, not something that happens in Broad Harbour.'

'Really?' Rora looked at him with disgust or impatience, Cameron couldn't quite tell which. 'You've seen yourself in the mirror. How do you explain it?'

Cameron turned away, staring into the night and hoping the darkness would blot out what he remembered of that reflection in the laboratory window.

'I'm not sure what I saw.'

'Yeah, right. Welcome to denial.' Rora hopped off the bench and landed in front of him. 'We've all been there, Cameron. And you know what? After a month or two, you can't argue with the truth any more and you learn to accept what you are. But you, you're special. And I'm sorry but you don't get the luxury of time. You have to wake up and accept what you are now.'

'Huh.' That sounded like a raw deal to Cameron.

'And if you really need more proof, here it

is.' Rora glanced left and right, as though making sure there were no passers-by to catch sight of something they shouldn't.

And then she changed.

It was like watching a werewolf movie. Rora's already-dark eyes deepened to solid black and her fine auburn hair grew rapidly, thickening to fur all over her morphing features. Her fingers flexed and stretched, scalpel-sharp claws snicking out of the tips. Her mouth swelled and she peeled back her lips to reveal a serious set of fangs. She was still very much human-shaped, but there was more of the fox about her now than ever.

'There now,' she said. 'That's something you can't argue with.'

She was right, Cameron was lost for words. All he could do was stare at her while his brain struggled to catch up with his eyes.

'And before you ask – no, I don't have a tail.'

For a moment Rora eyeballed Cameron. Then, almost imperceptibly, her mouth twitched into a grin, and Cameron found himself smiling for the first time since he had woken in the lab. It felt strange, as if his face had forgotten how to do it, but there was a funny sense of relief at the same time, even if it did hurt his stitches.

'So,' he said finally. 'Fox. Bloodhounds.' He gestured around the park. 'Are you expecting a load of toffs in red jackets to come jumping over the hedge on horses?'

Rora's smile faded. 'This isn't a joke, Cameron.'

'I know,' he replied. 'But if all this is true – what you said about me being the first of a new batch – then there could be more people like me.' Cameron pictured a face exactly like the one he had seen in that reflection. 'More monsters.'

'Well, I guess we know which one of you is the brains of this outfit.'

Cameron's heart skipped a beat.

He and Rora spun round simultaneously to face the figure standing in the shadows between the trees. The shape was little more than a silhouette, but Cameron knew who it was. He'd know her voice anywhere.

'Marie?'

Part of him wanted to rush forward and give her a huge hug, but something stopped him. In the chaos of his visit home and their flight to the park, he had forgotten about her again, and he felt another hot flood of shame. Until now, he'd had no idea she was even alive. Would she understand if he told her how crazy things had been?

She stepped lightly towards him, her movements as graceful as ever, and Cameron suddenly felt ugly and self-conscious, wishing he could hide his hideous new face. Then he remembered – Marie had been standing just behind him when the explosion happened. She must have been hurt too.

'Are you all right?'

'I'm fine. I'm better than fine.'

Marie's voice was soft, but there was something in the way she spoke that unsettled Cameron. As she got closer, he prayed that she was telling the truth; that she wasn't hurt or scarred.

Marie stepped into the light.

She had lost her lovely hair, he could see that much. It was close-cropped – like a soldier's – and he thought he could pick out the ridgeline of a scar on the side of her head. She was wearing combat trousers and a short vest that showed off her slender waist.

Coming up close to him, Marie took hold of both his hands and tilted her head towards him. Cameron gazed into her face, and suddenly he knew that everything was going to be all right.

Marie smiled her beautiful smile.

'Reckon you can fly, Reilly?'

And then she hurled him halfway across the park.

chapter seven

school reunion

Cameron crashed into a tree, the impact knocking the wind out of him. But it was nothing compared to the blow he'd been dealt on hearing those words. It had been Marie's voice, but the words had belonged unmistakably to Carl Monkton. Cameron had heard him use them at the power plant. But why would Marie be repeating them now?

Cameron was still struggling to make sense of it when Marie came striding over. Rora chased after her and made a diving tackle for her legs, but despite the fox-girl's light-footed steps, Marie must have heard her, because she spun round, kicking out to send Rora's small frame flying.

Cameron rose to his feet, but by the time he was up, Marie was right there in front of him again. Her fist shot out and punched him in the face, hard. Cameron staggered backwards, tasting blood. He touched a finger to his mouth.

'What are you doing, Marie? What's going on?'

Cameron's brain couldn't process what was happening. It was Marie he was looking at, but she'd never been violent. And certainly never so strong. He glanced past her to see Rora getting to her feet, clutching her side.

'Dr Fry wants a word with you,' said Marie.

'OK. That's good. I was just thinking I might turn myself in,' lied Cameron, stalling for time.

'Coming back with your tail between your legs?' sneered Marie. 'That figures. What a wuss – you make me puke.' She mimed sticking her fingers in her mouth. 'I don't know why Dr Fry wants you back, but he does. So I think

I'll just keep batting you in his general direction.'

Marie punched him again, square on the jaw. As Cameron reeled away, she grabbed hold of his shoulders, slammed him back against the tree, and drove her knee into his stomach. He struggled to get his arms up to push her off, but she locked an iron grip around his wrist, then wedged her forearm up under his chin, pinning him in place. She thrust her beautiful face into his and he finally got a good look at her eyes. They were cold, like steel.

Marie's eyes and not Marie's eyes.

Cameron's mind raced. Perhaps as well as enhancing Marie's body with superhuman strength, Fry had done something to her mind. Hypnosis, maybe. Something that was making her talk and act like Carl. But even so, there had to be something left of Marie inside. Surely he could get through to her?

He could feel her arm against his throat, squeezing his windpipe closed.

'Marie . . .' he choked.

'*Marie*. Oh, *Marie*,' she whined, mocking him, and gave a horrible laugh. 'I've got news for you, buddy. Dr Fry gave your girlfriend a new personality. Mine!'

Cameron's stomach lurched sickeningly. It couldn't be true. Surely even Dr Fry wasn't twisted enough to put one person's mind in another person's body? It wasn't possible. But even as he recoiled from the thought, part of Cameron's brain was telling him that was precisely what had happened with Carl and Marie.

Marie smirked, tapping the side of her head. 'Even if she was still in here, she wouldn't touch you with a bargepole now, Reilly. What happened to Mr Good Looking? Do you know how many people Dr Fry had to use to stitch you together? You're a walking school reunion.'

Cameron gritted his teeth, trying to force his one free arm up and lever her off.

'Yeah?' he gasped defiantly. 'Well, at least I don't have to use the girls' toilets.'

That hit a nerve. With a roar, Marie – Carl?

– lashed out. Latching onto Cameron, she hurled him through the air again.

Cameron landed in a heap. He was getting fed up with being thrown around. Grimacing, he flipped himself back onto his feet, braced to fight back. His opponent came at him with renewed enthusiasm, wearing a corrupted version of Marie's smile, as if relishing the prospect of a scrap.

She lashed out with a lightning-fast karate punch, then another. Like in his fight with the Bloodhounds, Cameron's body seemed to respond automatically, throwing up his arms to block. But somehow Marie's fists snuck in past his guard, as if she knew where his parries were going to come from before he did.

Cameron felt his fists clenching, all set to throw a punch of his own. But then he looked over at his enemy.

Marie's face stared back at him. How could he possibly hit her?

Forcing his arms down, Cameron backed up, trying to get quicker with his parries instead, doing anything he could think of to keep Marie at bay. She kept advancing, though, punishing him with another flurry of punches to the body, followed by a casual yet devastating spinning kick.

Cameron sailed backwards and landed in an untidy pile. Once more he hauled himself up off the grass as Marie came after him. Suddenly Rora appeared from nowhere and leaped between them, but Marie swatted her aside with a backhand blow that sent the fox-girl sprawling again. It was no good, Cameron was going to have to start getting creative or aggressive. Or both. Keeping his distance as best he could, he beat a fighting retreat across the park.

Scooping up a large rock from one of the flowerbeds, he hurled it in Marie's direction. Without breaking stride, she deflected the missile with a casual flick of her wrist. An old log was dispatched the same way, exploding in a shower of rotten wood; she ducked swiftly under a swung branch. Soon Cameron was hurling park benches between them, even uprooting a lamp-post and trying to fend her off with that. But Marie evaded or parried everything he threw her way.

And still she kept coming.

Cameron couldn't believe that just a few minutes earlier he'd been comparing himself with a superhero. He wasn't feeling much like one now. Or if he was, he had more than met his match. Marie, or Carl, or whatever the two of them had become, was a monster and a half, both quicker and stronger than him. The ease with which she evaded Cameron's obstacles was crushing. Finally she swooped under another thrown park bench and it was back to hand-to-hand.

That was it. Cameron realized he wasn't getting a choice in the matter: it was hit back or be pummelled into the ground.

Marie swept at Cameron's legs with a kick, but he jumped just in time, and hit out with a tightly bunched fist. It smacked Marie on the chin, jerking her head backwards.

'That's more like it!' she said with a laugh, before launching herself at Cameron to repay him in kind.

Cameron reversed, ducking, and driving up with his fist. But she chopped the blow down. Back on her feet again, Rora suddenly came at Marie from the side, forcing her to turn and buying Cameron a window of opportunity to land some solid blows of his own.

For a moment Cameron and Rora had Marie on the defensive. Until Marie seized one of Rora's arms and flung her like a rag doll into one of the broken benches scattered around their battleground. Then she was back to facing Cameron solo, and dishing out bare-knuckle blows and roundhouse kicks.

Cameron didn't know how much more he could take, but he couldn't shake off the feeling that Marie was just playing with him, delivering two good kicks or punches for every one of his that made it through her own defences.

Worse, every time he did land a blow, she just cracked an evil grin, while he winced inwardly at the thought of hitting a girl. When his knuckles slammed into her nose, it should have been a small victory. Instead, all he got was a queasy feeling as he watched the blood trickling down over her lips. Marie just seemed to be spurred on.

Finally she jumped high in the air while Cameron was glancing around desperately for any sort of weapon to hold her back. She came down on top of him and slammed him to the ground, a hand at his throat. Slender fingers that Cameron had only known as gentle and tender dug into his neck like steel claws. Her other hand was raised, bunched into a fist.

Cameron threw up one arm to fend off the coming punch, while his other hand scrabbled to prise Marie's fingers off his throat. He could feel himself beginning to black out. Sickeningly, he could also feel something in his right arm beginning to revolve. He knew right away it was the gun that had put a smoking hole in that Bloodhound.

No!

Last-ditch defence or not, he wasn't having that weapon come out of him again. No matter what.

Above him, Marie seethed, pure hate gleaming in her eyes as she brought her fist down. Cameron twisted his head aside as far as he could and something in his skull clicked. Not like an idea lighting up – an actual, audible click.

Marie's body jerked. Sparks flashed and sizzled all over her as she was flung away. She landed not far from Cameron, twitching and convulsing on the grass. There was a faint whiff of ozone and singed hair, and Cameron glimpsed a tiny blue spark spitting from the end of the middle finger of his right hand.

Another weapon. Some kind of Taser, he guessed.

Relieved and disgusted in equal measure, he struggled to sit up. Marie's body was still jerking sporadically, but her eyes remained fixed on Cameron, burning with helpless rage.

'Finish it!' urged Rora, limping over, an ugly, vengeful expression on her face.

Cameron crawled towards Marie, leaning over his paralysed enemy.

'It', Rora had said, but Cameron only saw

'her'. The thing lying on the ground might have Carl's personality, but Cameron could only see Marie's face. Could he kill her? He imagined that he could feel the weight of the gun lurking inside his arm. That would do the trick, for sure.

But he'd already made up his mind. He was *not*, under any circumstances, letting that gun out again – not ever. He could still smell the smoke of it in his nostrils, and see the wound it had made. He couldn't do that again, least of all to Marie. He could hardly believe he'd forced himself to hit her.

No more.

'How did you find us?' Cameron demanded.

The sneer that crept across those familiar features did not belong to Marie. 'You've got a built-in tracking device, dumbo.'

Rora grabbed at Cameron's arm. 'Then we've got to get away. Now. Kill it! We don't have a lot of time!'

'Your new girlfriend's right,' said the thing that looked like Marie. 'The Hounds will be here any minute. Better kill me quick. If you've got the guts.'

Cameron stood and unclenched his fists, shaking his head.

Rora let out an exasperated yell. 'All right then! Leave a job half done! It'll come back and bite us all later. Let's go! We need to get under-ground.'

Grabbing hold of his hand, she tugged Cameron into a run as they heard the howls of the Bloodhounds breaking out all over the park.

Sprinting back towards the scooter, Rora flipped the cover off a nearby manhole and dived inside.

Cameron had no choice but to follow her down into the darkness.

chapter eight

the monster republic

As Cameron and Rora waded through the sewers, the shadows darkened to fit Cameron's mood. Try as he might, he couldn't shake off the horror of his encounter with Marie/Carl. The person he had most longed to see and the person he would happily never have seen again, all rolled into one. The latest twist in the waking nightmare he had been trapped in ever since he woke up in Dr Fry's laboratory.

The pair turned down yet another tunnel. There was no noise but the splash of their footsteps and the low, mechanical hiss of servos that now accompanied Cameron's every move, like a soundtrack he couldn't turn off. He was freezing, and his body ached from the beating he had received. On top of that, he was having to contend with the stench of drains and the nagging sense of a cold shoulder from his guide. Rora hadn't said a word since they'd got below ground.

Looked like it was up to him to start a conversation.

'Wherever you're taking me, I hope it doesn't stink like this.'

'Be glad you don't have a fox's sense of smell,' Rora snapped.

She didn't so much as glance round, and the anger in her voice was plain as a smack in the face.

'Hey, what's your problem?' Cameron demanded, picking up his pace to bring himself level with her. 'I'm the one who should be complaining. It's me who's had my whole life turned upside down. It's me who's been made into some sort of Frankenstein's Terminator. And it's my girlfriend back there who's had I don't know what done to her!'

His shouting voice echoed down the tunnel.

Rora stopped him with a shove to the chest and a shout of her own.

'My problem is you're still thinking of it as your girlfriend! It isn't. It's Dr Fry's newest recruit. You could have killed that thing! You had your chance right there. We might not get another one. Next time, while you're busy remembering what it was like to kiss her, that thing will kill you! And me, and any of my friends too, if it gets the chance! *That's* my problem!'

Her words bounced around the walls accusingly before fading into the darkness. Silence descended again, and the look on Rora's face suggested it couldn't last long enough as far as she was concerned.

She turned and marched off again, leaving Cameron little option but to follow. So much for his attempt to break the ice. The atmosphere as they slogged along was even colder than before.

The enforced silence made the long journey seem longer still, but eventually Rora led them out of the sewers and into a storm drain, the hint of a breeze reaching them from somewhere out of sight. It wasn't much of an improvement, but at least the stench faded a bit. Cameron still felt damp and miserable, but he reckoned that last feeling would be with him for a long time.

Looking around cautiously, Rora crossed the storm drain and trotted a few metres further along, until she was standing in front of a rusty metal door. She tilted her face upwards and Cameron spotted a small black box discreetly mounted above the door. With a spinning sensation, his eye zoomed in, giving him a close-up view.

A camera.

Through the wave of dizziness that seemed to accompany every newly discovered feature of his souped-up body, Cameron felt an unexpected sense of relief. So this republic of hers operated some rudimentary level of security. He guessed he should find that encouraging.

With a dull clank, the door opened, allowing Cameron and Rora through into what might have once been some sort of maintenance area, with electrical junction boxes and shelves along one wall. In the cramped space, a desk and chair had been set up. A handful of computer monitors showed different stretches of tunnel, including the one immediately outside. There was a single bed in the corner, with a shabby-looking blanket. A small boy, no more than eight years old, stood holding the door.

So, not the most sophisticated security setup in the world. But it probably did the job. After all, who on earth was going to be wandering casually down a storm drain to find this place by accident?

'Rora.' The kid gave her a brisk nod before returning to his seat. Cameron got a good look at him in the steady light from the monitor screens: he was pasty-faced, with freckles where his skin showed between a polished metal skull cap and a crude steel jaw.

Cameron tensed instinctively – the boy looked a little too much like a Bloodhound for his liking. Almost immediately, he felt bad.

After all, his own face was no longer exactly going to inspire trust. He gave a nod, but the boy's eyes were already glued back on the empty screens. Whoever he was, he was dedicated to his job.

'That's Guard,' said Rora quietly. 'He's our doorkeeper. And in case you're wondering – yeah, he was part of the Bloodhound project. But he's very much on our side. He likes to keep watch, so that suits everyone.'

And provides a measure of additional security, thought Cameron. If anyone did wander down here by chance, the sight of this boy would certainly send them running.

Rora headed straight for a ladder hanging down through a hole in the ceiling. Cameron climbed awkwardly after her.

'So what's his story? He's always down here?'

'No, he has a nap from time to time, and someone else takes a turn at the monitors. But really, he's the best. No eyes in the back of his head, but a lot of other sensors packed in where half his brain used to be.'

Cameron shook his head, wondering how Rora could be so casual about something so out of the ordinary.

At the top of the ladder, Rora pushed back a grating and they both clambered up into a dimly lit, brick-walled passage. It led through into a low-ceilinged chamber with a slightly dank feel. It seemed to have been set up as some sort of common room. A mix of chairs and tables – from plastic garden seats and ragged-looking armchairs to large trestles and weighty, woodworm-riddled dining tables – occupied most of the central area, while a number of bunks were squeezed into narrow spaces up against the walls. Cameron couldn't avoid the impression he'd escaped one cellar just to come and live in another.

'Cosy,' he remarked quietly.

'There are more rooms,' Rora told him brusquely.

Indeed, Cameron could already see several corridors and doorways leading off from this main room. Through one, he could make out a handful of kids clustered in front of a TV, watching a movie with the sound turned down low.

One of them happened to glance in their direction.

'Hey, it's Rora!'

Everyone in the room was up on their feet in an instant, rushing over to surround the fox-girl, patting her on the shoulder or giving her a quick hug. The youngest looked about seven or eight; the oldest, around Cameron's age. With some, it was hard to tell their age through the fur or scales that covered their bodies. Others, more like Cameron or Guard, had mechanical components welded or stitched onto them, bursting out of their arms, faces or – as Cameron saw when one turned to flick off the TV – backs.

The Monster Republic was well named. None of these kids could ever pass as normal, ever go out in public without attracting attention and alarm. But that didn't seem to bother them here. In response to the warm shout, more kids were appearing in other doorways and filing in to offer their own welcomes. The hall reverberated with calls of 'You made it!' and 'Good to see you!' It was a real homecoming.

For Rora, anyway.

Finally she freed herself from the throng. 'Everyone – this is Cameron.'

As one, the assembled monsters turned their attention to him.

Silence fell like a lead weight.

Some of the crowd stared openly, their looks filled with tension. Others stole wary glances out of the corners of their eyes, then looked away when Cameron tried to catch their gaze. Nobody moved or spoke, but the air was charged, like before a fight.

Cameron shifted uneasily. Did he look that bad to them, then? Or was there something else going on? When Rora had told him about the Monster Republic, he'd imagined . . . Well, he didn't know exactly what he had imagined, but something better than this. Somewhere people didn't judge you by your appearance, for starters.

It looked as if Rora sensed his discomfort

and shared it, because she clapped her hands briskly.

'All right,' she said, with strained cheerfulness. 'We'll do proper introductions later. First things first. Cameron's wired with a tracking device. It won't work under ground, but we still need to get it out. Slater, can you take him to see Tinker, please?'

Before Cameron could open his mouth to object, a dark-haired boy of about his own age stepped forward. He had sharp features and a muscular torso mounted on bulky mechanical legs that bent the wrong way, like a dog's hind legs. His lip curled unpleasantly, and he looked as unhappy about having to escort Cameron as Cameron felt about being handed over to him.

Slater wordlessly jerked his thumb towards a door. As Cameron walked towards it, everyone else in the room backed away as if he had the plague, clearing a path ahead of him. He lowered his head and stomped through, into a narrow corridor, biting his tongue as he went.

Slater led him down the corridor and into a side room jam-packed with desks piled high with jumbled equipment, like some sort of electronics lab. In the middle of the chaos sat an old leather dentist's chair, with a collection of cables and wires running off it.

A small boy with spiky blond hair and glasses popped into view from behind the chair, where he had been fussing with some of the electrics. Of all the faces Cameron had seen so far, this kid's features were the most normal. But they twitched spasmodically, as if he was being electrocuted. His whole body was constantly in motion: his head jerking this way and that; his eyes flicking about like a bird's, focusing on something different every second.

Although never on Cameron's face . . .

Slater marched Cameron over to the chair and patted the seat with a twisted smile. As he sat, Slater looked down at him for an instant as if he was a bad smell, before turning back to the other kid.

'He's bugged, Tink. See what you can do. Don't worry, I'll be just outside.' Then he marched out.

The twitchy kid moved in closer, his lips moving. Even with his enhanced hearing, Cameron could only just make out what he was muttering to himself.

'Divinity Project, Subject Number Five-Oh-One. Human cyborg. Partial titanium exoskeleton. Internal power supply. Weapons capability unknown.'

Cameron gritted his teeth. *Good to meet you too, Tinker – my name's Cameron*, he thought bitterly.

With a look of intense concentration on his always-moving face, Tinker rummaged through some of the tools on the nearest desk. He pulled out a large, vaguely gun-shaped device, which he began to run over Cameron's head and torso.

As he did so, Cameron noticed that while Tinker's face was still a mass of tics and twitches, his hands were suddenly as steady as rocks. When the scanner reached Cameron's right shoulder, it suddenly started emitting frantic bleeps.

'Automatic tracking device,' muttered Tinker. 'Internally mounted.'

He nodded, entirely to himself, and reached for another tool. Then, without a word, he pulled down the neck of Cameron's T-shirt and flipped open a panel on his shoulder, the new instrument poised to begin poking around inside.

'Hey!' snarled Cameron, leaping to his feet with clenched fists. 'What do you think you're doing? I'm not just some faulty toaster!'

Tinker backpedalled, knocking a pile of equipment to the floor with a crash. He stared directly at Cameron for the first time, his wide, scared eyes blinking rapidly, while his facial muscles went into all sorts of new spasms.

'Keep your tools to yourself!' Cameron shouted.

In a flash, Slater was inside the room.

'What did you do?' he demanded, squaring up to Cameron.

'Nothing,' snapped Cameron. 'It was *him.*'

'What's going on here?'

Rora stood in the doorway, hands on hips.

'He attacked Tinker,' replied Slater, his eyes never leaving Cameron.

'N-n-no, he didn't,' stammered Tinker. 'It was m-m-my fault.'

'What happened?'

Cameron scowled. 'He started messing with my arm.'

Rora sighed impatiently. 'How else do you think he's going to get the bug out? Were you expecting him to say, "This won't hurt a bit"?' Her sarcasm stung.

'I didn't come here for this,' growled Cameron. Even as he spoke, he knew it was a feeble line. He wasn't sure why he had come here.

'I'd sit still if I were you. Tinker knows what he's doing. Tinker always knows what he's doing – and we need that thing out of you as soon as possible. Trust me.'

Cameron rolled his good eye, but sat back down anyway. There didn't seem to be a lot of choice.

'And you can go, Slater,' continued Rora. 'I don't think Tinker really needs your help. I'll stay.'

For a moment Slater glared at Rora, chewing the inside of his cheek, as if biting back words he really wanted to speak. Then he turned on his metal heel and left. Cameron felt himself relax. He realized that his hands were still bunched into fists. If Rora hadn't shown up, he didn't know what might have happened.

Cameron turned back to Tinker, who met his gaze briefly and gave a nervous, flickering smile.

'Hi,' he said. 'Is it O-O-OK if I . . .'

Cameron nodded curtly.

With the calm dexterity of a surgeon, Tinker picked up the tools he had dropped, and began fishing around in Cameron's shoulder. It was a strange sensation. Cameron was aware of something moving inside him, but there was no pain.

While Tinker worked, Cameron kept silent, telling himself that it was all for the best. But he couldn't shake off a nagging sense of doubt. So far, the Monster Republic wasn't working out to be so great. Apart from the fact that he was being worked on by a twitchy kid instead of a real doctor, he wasn't sure it was all that different from Fry's laboratory.

'D-d-done,' said Tinker. He plopped a tiny capsule into a metal dish, then hastened off without another word before Cameron could even say thank you.

'Gone to feed it to a stray cat, maybe?' said Cameron. 'That'd throw the Bloodhounds a false trail.'

Rora smiled tightly. 'Yeah. Maybe.'

Cameron sat up. 'We need to talk—'

The fox-girl shook her head. 'You need to get some rest.'

She led him back into the corridor. Sticking her head through a door for a quick inspection, she ushered him into a side room almost completely filled by a bunk bed. From the size of the place, Cameron guessed it might once have been a store cupboard. There was no one else there.

'This should do you. Top or bottom, whichever you prefer,' she said, gesturing at the bed. Cameron opened his mouth to speak, but Rora cut him off.

'We'll talk tomorrow. Get some rest. I need some, even if you don't.'

Cameron remembered what she had said in the park about her weakness being a lack of stamina. She certainly looked tired now. Maybe he'd get more answers from her in the morning. He slumped down on the bottom bunk, which creaked alarmingly under the weight of his new body.

'Not quite the warm welcome I was led to expect,' he said pointedly. 'Most of your friends out there won't even look me in the eye.'

'There you go again. Not everything's about *you*,' Rora replied. 'This is strange for them too. Give them time.'

'Huh. If you say so.' Cameron didn't buy it.

Rora shook her head and left. Moodily, Cameron settled back and planted his head on the pillow. He didn't suppose for a minute he'd be able to sleep, but maybe he ought to try. He stared up at the underside of the top bunk for a moment, then sighed. *Get some rest*. That was easy for her to say.

How was he supposed to close his electronic eye?

Ruefully he had to admit he didn't have a clue. Perhaps Rora had dealt with enough similar people to tell him the answer. It would mean having to ask for her help, though. Again.

Embarrassed, Cameron slipped off the bed. Sticking his head through the door, he opened his mouth to call after her.

There was no need. Rora was standing just a few metres down the corridor, flanked by the technical whizz-kid, Tinker, and the sour-faced figure of Slater, who looked as moody and sullen as Cameron felt. They were talking in low, urgent voices.

Before Cameron could 'turn up' his hearing, Slater spotted him, and placed a warning hand on Rora's arm. But really, Cameron didn't need to hear what they were saying. Everything about the trio, from their sudden pointed silence to their furtive glances towards him, made it obvious.

They were talking about him. Great.

Rora cleared her throat. 'Do you need anything?'

Cameron gave her a long hard look.

'No.'

Throwing himself back on the bed, he rolled over to stare at the brick wall. He didn't know if sleep would come, but he hoped it would, and soon. Otherwise there was a long night ahead. A night of just lying there, thinking about everything he had lost: his home, his family, everyone he really cared about. His whole life.

chapter nine

coming to terms

Next morning, Cameron woke feeling rotten.

He had lain awake for what felt like hours, his mind churning. When sleep had finally come, it had been like dozing in front of the TV, electronics buzzing away in a constant background hiss of static. Vague images had flashed through his mind – Marie, the Bloodhounds, Dr Fry – but nothing he could hold onto and call a proper dream. Now he was awake his body felt rested, but his mind was as confused as ever.

Cameron wondered why Dr Fry hadn't wired his subjects so they didn't need sleep at all. It seemed a sensible thing to do if you wanted to create some sort of super-soldiers. Maybe he was working on it. But anyway, lack of sleep wasn't his real problem.

No, what was bugging Cameron most was the fact that all the questions that had kept him awake throughout the night were still with him in the morning, like a chesty cough that he couldn't dislodge. Despite their endless cycling, they had gone nowhere. He couldn't think his way through them.

Maybe he could try talking. Speaking about his feelings wasn't something Cameron enjoyed, but some of the monsters he'd seen the night before looked like they might have undergone similar 'treatment' at the hands of Dr Fry. Maybe they would understand how he felt.

Cameron strained his enhanced hearing. Silence. No murmurs, no movements. The safe house sounded deserted. Rora had promised to take him somewhere where there were other people like him, but here he was, back on his own. With a sigh, Cameron got up and went looking for the bathroom. He found it quickly, but he had barely got through the door when he stopped dead. He should have expected it, but the sight was still a shock.

There was a mirror above the sink.

Well, he did need a proper look at what had been done to him. If that didn't wake him up, nothing would. Maybe that first time he'd seen himself in the lab window, shock had made his face seem worse than it was. Maybe shock had made his family react so badly. Maybe a second, more patient look now – now that he was prepared – would reveal a better picture.

Deliberately avoiding a glance at the mirror, Cameron dipped his head towards the sink, ran the tap and splashed a couple of handfuls of water on his face.

And froze. Maybe he shouldn't have done that.

Cameron waited for the flash, the cascade of sparks and the jolt of electricity, but nothing happened.

He breathed a sigh of relief. There was so much to think about, so much to consider. New rules about how to go about everyday life

– whole new minefields. Luckily it looked as if his new electronic eye was waterproof. That was something.

Unable to put off the moment any longer, Cameron slowly raised his head and gazed at his reflection in the mirror. The glass wasn't exactly spotless but it was a much sharper image than he'd got in the lab window.

Sharper – and more shocking.

A walking school reunion. Marie had been telling the truth. His face was a patchwork of bruises and scars, various features crudely stitched together. Just as she had taunted him the night before, Cameron had clearly been cobbled together from several bodies. That realization, as well as the portrait in the mirror, made him feel sick.

Worse – much worse – he began to recognize some of the pieces.

In the midst of the last night's madness, Cameron hadn't had time to think about what had happened to the rest of his class. Now, in the cold light of day, he was finding out. The horrible irony of it was that he had clearly been one of the lucky ones. One of the survivors.

Some of the others had not been so fortunate.

One ear and the top left-hand quarter of Cameron's face was now black. From his first glimpse back in the lab, he had thought it was just badly bruised. Now he could see that it had once belonged to Kwame, the Nigerian boy who sat next to him in maths. Livid scars joined the dark skin to the rest of his face and, as Cameron reached up to touch it, he saw from the bitten nails that two of the fingers on his good hand had come from Tony, who played in goal on the football team.

Retching, Cameron leaned forward to be sick into the sink, but nothing came out. He closed his eyes, unable to look at himself again.

How many more pieces of his body had once belonged to his friends? Or even kids he'd only known to wave at from across the playing field? Discovering his new machine parts had been bad enough, but this was worse. These scraps of human flesh had once been attached to living, breathing boys – boys like him – until they had been grafted onto Cameron by some twisted butcher of a surgeon.

No wonder even the other monsters had shunned him. How could they know who he was, when Cameron himself couldn't tell any more? Whatever Rora said, he didn't belong here.

He turned away in disgust and strode out of the room – and all but collided with a slight figure coming the other way. It was a small boy. His eyes, hidden behind sunglasses, were about level with Cameron's chest. If he was trying to look cool, though, he was trying way too hard. The shades didn't really suit the gloomy subterranean lighting.

'Smarts,' the boy said, and it took Cameron a moment to realize he was introducing himself. He held out a large pumpkin as if it was some sort of award. 'You must be Cameron. Welcome. Could you help me with this?'

Cameron took the pumpkin automatically,

looking at it as if it might go off like a bomb. What was this? Some sort of Halloween joke?

But instead of chuckling to himself or even waiting to see the look on Cameron's face, Smarts headed off down the corridor. Nonplussed, and not sure what to say to the first person who wasn't treating him like some kind of invader, Cameron trailed after him, and soon found himself in a basic kitchen. Smarts was already sitting in a large chair strung from the ceiling, polishing his dark glasses. He put them on the worktop in front of him and gestured over at one of the sideboards.

'The knives are over there,' he said. 'And a chopping board – unless someone's helpfully put it away somewhere it doesn't belong.' He smiled. 'Dinner. There's a rota. But every time my turn comes round, I always end up having to get help.'

'Why?' asked Cameron, half a second before he realized the answer. Smarts's hand was fumbling across the worktop in search of his sunglasses, his unfocused eyes staring at a point somewhere over Cameron's shoulder.

Smarts smiled again as his fingertips found the glasses and slipped them on.

'Ah, you've noticed. It's the sharp intake of breath that always gives it away. You're quick, though. It takes most people much longer.'

Cameron moved to the counter-top and set the pumpkin down. He picked up a knife, feeling like carving a really ugly face in it. So that explained why Smarts was being friendly: it was easier to avoid judging by appearances when you couldn't see.

'Oh, don't worry,' said Smarts as Cameron started cutting into the vegetable. 'I know all about you. Well, all about what you are since Dr Fry got hold of you.'

Cameron peered over his shoulder, wondering if the boy had some sort of mind-reading ability. His expression appeared entirely innocent and amiable.

'You'll have to fill me in on the rest some time. If you like.'

'Or if *you* like,' Cameron countered. 'I don't get the impression many people here want to hear my story.'

'Ah, yes. The thing is, not everyone was in favour of rescuing you, which is why some of them are a bit standoffish. You're the first non-Reject to be brought into the Republic. Even by our standards, you're unique. They don't know what to make of you. Some of them are still worried you might betray us.'

'Great,' said Cameron. 'So even the Rejects reject me.' He went back to hacking at the pumpkin.

'Yes, well, they don't all see things as clearly as I do.'

Cameron looked round again. For a moment Smarts deadpanned, giving nothing away, then his mouth spread into an impish grin. Cameron smiled back. It was hard to stay grumpy with a blind boy cracking sight jokes.

'Where did you get the pumpkin from?' he asked.

'One of the foraging groups found it in an

abandoned allotment,' replied Smarts. 'That's what everyone else is out doing.'

'Foraging for food?' asked Cameron incredulously.

'How else do you think we get it?' Smarts said patiently. 'It's not as if we can just walk into the supermarket. Although' – he lowered his voice conspiratorially – 'we have been known to make after-hours visits.'

'Break in, you mean?'

'Yup.' Smarts smiled. 'Tinker disables the alarm and hacks into the camera system, then the others move in and help themselves. The CCTV footage shows nothing, but when the manager opens up next morning, the shelves are empty. Leaves a lot of security firms scratching their heads, I can tell you!'

Cameron shook his head. He hadn't stopped to think about how the monsters survived from day to day without the resources available to normal people. He was starting to see that just putting enough food on the table every day would be a struggle, but the Republic had to find shelter and technical equipment too. And all in secret.

Cameron opened his mouth to ask Smarts how he had come to be part of the Monster Republic in the first place, but at that moment Rora walked in.

'Hey, Smarts,' she said, but crossed straight to Cameron. 'I've arranged a special meeting of the Republic for this afternoon.'

Cameron almost shrugged.

Great. But what's that got to do with me?

He realized that he was still annoyed with her for last night, and now again for interrupting.

If Rora noticed his displeasure, she didn't react.

'Before then, I think it's time we tested your abilities. See what you're really capable of.'

Yeah, thought Cameron. *See how useful I can be, more like.*

He flashed her the knife. 'I can cut vegetables.'

Rora laughed. 'That's vital around here. But

Smarts can find someone else to help out. Right, Smarts?'

'Sure.'

Cameron slapped the knife down. 'Lead the way then.'

Rora steered him out of the kitchen and down along a passage Cameron hadn't had the chance to explore. As she led him through a door, he asked her, 'So what's the story with Smarts?'

Rora regarded him with surprise. 'I'd have thought that was pretty obvious. It's in the name.' She tapped the side of her head. 'He's got lots going on up here – enhanced intelligence. He's brilliant at chess too. He'll beat you and everyone else in the Republic. At the same time.'

She continued through the doorway, and down another stretch of passage. Cameron followed, shaking his head at the irony of it all. The closest thing he had found to a friend so far in this Monster Republic was a chess geek.

That would never have happened at school.

chapter ten
testing time

Rora ushered Cameron ahead of her into another windowless room set up as a rudimentary gym. There were crash mats on the floor, a few weights and climbing bars fixed to one wall, and a punch bag hanging in the corner. She followed him inside and closed the door behind them.

Cameron turned and looked at Rora. 'You want me to work out?'

'Eventually. We need to know what you can do.'

He shrugged. 'Well, apparently I can just about hold a pair of mechanical crushers apart. I know judo or kung fu, or something. I can see in the dark. And I can – I don't know – filter sounds, decide which ones I want to listen to.'

'Right.' Rora nodded, showing no surprise. She had seen most of those capabilities at first hand. 'Also, there was that death-defying jump down the stairwell. And I see your injuries from that scrap last night have started healing already.'

Cameron glanced down at himself. He could barely see any scrapes or bruises – and the metal parts of him were scarcely scratched or dented. And yet he knew he had taken a heck of a battering from the creature that had looked so like Marie.

'You think there might be more?'

It was Rora's turn to shrug. 'Well, I think we ought to find out.'

Cameron stood there feeling awkward. He used to love PE at school, but this was entirely different. And he didn't like the idea of Rora watching and awarding him marks out of ten.

'What would you like me to do first?

Press-ups?' He gestured at the punch bag. 'Kick the stuffing out of that?'

'Nope.' Rora approached to within a couple of paces and stood with her hands on her hips. 'I'll be your punch bag for now.'

Cameron laughed, but Rora's expression didn't change. She was being serious.

'No, thanks. I don't like hitting girls.'

'Yeah, I saw that last night. But you're going to have to get used to it, because Fry has made a monster out of your girlfriend's body. Your ex-girlfriend, by the way. That's something else you're going to have to get used to.'

Cameron glared at her. 'What did he do to her, anyway? Fry?'

Rora shrugged. 'How should I know? Straightforward brain transplant would be my guess.'

'Brain transplant? That's . . . stupid.' The idea of Carl's brain being put in Marie's head. It was the maddest thing Cameron had heard yet. And anyway, he'd never figured Carl had much of a brain in the first place.

'Depends.' Rora smirked. 'If she was as

much of a dumb blonde as she looked, it might have been an upgrade.'

Cameron blinked, wanting to believe he'd misheard her. Involuntarily his fist clenched.

'Don't talk about her like that!'

'What if she turns up again and kicks you around some more?' Rora pressed. 'Are you going to stand there and take it? How are you ever going to hit *her* face if you can't even hit *mine*? She doesn't exist any more, Cameron. She's dead. However it was done, Marie's not home. Someone else has moved in.'

Cameron's anger flashed. Why did she have to be so harsh?

'Besides,' Rora assured him, 'you'll never be able to hit me anyway. Not if your life depended on it.'

She started to bounce on her feet, dancing lightly around him. Cameron watched her furiously. Sure, she was goading him, but there was no way he was going to punch her.

A furred hand flashed out, almost too fast for him to see, and slapped him on the face. Rora went on dancing.

'Hey!'

Again, a blur of motion and a ringing slap. She was seriously quick. The skin of Cameron's cheek stung hotly. Growling, he warned her, 'Do that one more time—'

She did. Only this time, her hand lashed out and yanked his ear.

Cameron threw out an arm to bat her hand aside, but it was already gone. And Rora was gone too, skipping behind him.

He spun to face her. She smacked him on the nose.

'Ow!'

Right, that was it. She was going to get her wish.

Cameron snapped out a punch. Without even moving her feet, Rora weaved her head, snakelike, out of his reach. He swung a second time – but she wasn't there. A winding blow to the kidneys told him she was behind him again.

He spun and nearly caught her a backhand slap, forcing the fox-girl into a less dignified duck.

'Getting better,' she said.

They fought on, Cameron getting flashbacks to last night and his hopeless fight against Marie. Rora, like her, was clearly quicker than he was. Maybe that was a female thing – deadlier than the male and all that. The main difference, though, was that despite the embarrassing ease with which Rora seemed to penetrate his defences, Cameron found himself enjoying this challenge. That and the fact that when he finally managed to clock Rora one, unlike Marie, the fox-girl was knocked flat on her back.

'Are you OK?' he said, leaning towards her.

With an athletic pirouette, Rora leaped into the air, her foot connecting with Cameron's head in a spinning kick that left his ears ringing.

'You'll have to do better than that,' she snarled.

Facing off, they carried on sparring until Cameron had landed another three or four hits on her. Infuriating as it was, trying to make the punches connect, he eased up with each one, recognizing that despite her bravado, he might actually do her some serious damage.

And he was getting quicker. It was as if his reflexes, although never quite matching hers, were improving all the time, adjusting to their new-found performance levels. As though his body was learning. Rora was finding it harder and harder to hit him, while he was finding it ever easier to hit her. Eventually, after a thump to her ribs that had her bent over and Cameron looking on with genuine concern, Rora called it quits.

'I'll be fine.' She covered her grimace with a smile and waved him off. 'Honestly. I asked for it. Plus, like I said, you need to tone down the compassion anyway. I'm more concerned with toughening you up than I am about my ribs.' She stood up straight. 'All right. Next up – missile defence.'

'Excuse me?'

Rora walked to the other side of the room, signalling Cameron to stay put. Then, without warning, she stooped to pick up a brick and flung it at him.

Cameron yelled, 'Hey!'

But even as he did so, his eyes flickered dizzyingly and his view was suddenly overlaid with a kind of digital display, like on a flight simulator computer game. A moving circle of green light traced the path of the brick coming towards him, while numbers also flashed up, calculating the distance. The display's sudden appearance threw him for a split-second – but, on impulse, Cameron's hand shot out and deflected the missile off to the right.

'Oh, wow,' he breathed. As well as the tracking system, now Cameron could see menus and icons on the edge of his peripheral vision, hinting at more unknown skills hidden just out of sight.

Without pausing, Rora chucked another brick towards him. Then another, straight at his head.

'Wait! What do you—?'

There was no time to complain. The bricks came faster and faster. As much as he wanted to tell Rora to stop, instead Cameron switched to some sort of automatic defensive mode, half his mind tracking the trajectories of the bricks flashing up on the display, the other half directing his limbs into reflex deflections or dodges. If anything, the faster the bricks came at him, the better he responded. As if the less he thought about them consciously, the more effective his skills became. Finally, he met the last brick with a karate chop, and it broke apart in mid-air, the pieces falling to the floor with a thud.

Cameron was as breathless with excitement as he was from the exercise. Regardless of all the cruel things that had been done to him, he couldn't help but start to see the possibilities – and explanations.

'So that's how Marie deflected everything I threw at her last night!' A sudden thought deflated him. 'But wait, she already knew how to do all that. And she sure as hell had an edge over me. What else can she do that I can't?'

Rora gave him a consoling pat on the shoulder. 'Don't sweat it. Listen, the thing you have to bear in mind is that Fry will have told his pet all about its abilities. He'll have trained it, and made sure it was aware of all its capabilities.' She flopped down on an exercise mat. 'Anyway, you're the same model, so it makes sense that the two of you will have mostly the same abilities. Similar enhancements. You'll just have to learn to use yours on your own. And practice is the best way to do that.'

'Great,' said Cameron. Still, he did feel encouraged.

With a faint whine of servos, he sat down beside Rora, but she was up again almost immediately and heading for the door. 'I need a shower,' she said over her shoulder. 'Be time for the meeting soon.'

'All right. See you there, I guess.'

Cameron felt a twinge of disappointment that she hadn't stopped to talk. But he shrugged it off. As much as he probably needed a shower himself, he settled down to explore more aspects of his visual display.

It was kind of like navigating a powerful computer system when you had no idea what it was for: exciting and unnerving at the same time. Of course, there was no keyboard to tap, no mouse to click – and no Help menu. Instead, to activate a particular function or access a file, Cameron had to focus his attention on an icon or area of the display, and then the best way he could describe it was to 'think at it'.

Experimenting like that, within a few minutes Cameron had discovered that the system was called a Head-Up Display, and boasted a number of cool features. He quickly found the Taser activator that would allow him to operate the weapon whenever he wanted, rather than having to wait for it to trigger automatically in an emergency. There was also interfacing software that would allow him to connect with a wide range of computer networks through ports in the fingers of his mechanical arm. He even had a built-in mobile phone, although the HUD unsurprisingly revealed a signal strength of zero here below ground.

Finally, with a wry smile, Cameron found a satellite navigation system. Life was full of simple ironies like that, he supposed. Among all his other weird and wonderful 'enhancements', he had a system that could fix his position on the globe to within a metre, but couldn't begin to tell him his place in the world.

The meeting took place in the common room. Most of the tables had been pushed back to the walls, and all the chairs – simple plastic ones and big old armchairs alike – had been arranged in rows facing one end, like a rather eccentric classroom. Around thirty kids had gathered, some of them still chatting before taking their seats.

There were some with furry faces, a couple with leathery hides who resembled pigs, one whose entire face had been replaced with a tinted visor, plenty with mechanical limbs, some with armour plating. There was even one girl who was positively reptilian, with a flickering tongue and a scaly skin that shifted colours. Cameron didn't feel like looking too closely at any of them, and hoped they weren't looking at him either.

He could sense the tension in the room as

Rora led him up one side of the rows of chairs towards a table that had been positioned at the front, where the teacher's desk would have been. As if he was something she was about to show off to class.

Biting his tongue, Cameron said nothing, keeping his head down so that his eyes didn't have to focus on individual 'monsters' as he passed them. He knew their stares would be filled with the same mix of accusation and fear that he had seen in them the night before.

He took a seat and gazed hard at the table in front of him.

'Hi, everybody,' said Rora. 'Some of you saw him come in yesterday, but I'd like you all to meet Cameron properly. He's going to be a valuable member of the Republic.' She offered Cameron an encouraging smile that made him want to squirm with embarrassment.

Without waiting for an invitation, someone jumped to their feet. Cameron glanced up.

Dark hair, dark expression. Slater.

Cameron remembered him clearly from last night. If he remembered Cameron, he didn't show it. He didn't even look at him, but spoke to Rora instead.

'Before we get to the personal introductions, how do we even know he's safe? Huh?'

'Slater—' began Rora.

But he wasn't giving her a chance.

'He could still be under Fry's control. He could be working for him. But here you are, parading him in front of us like a long-lost brother. You've even given him a full tour of the place. Nice one, Rora. Have you lost your marbles?'

'Are you finished?' Rora eyed him severely. 'I've seen what he can do. With his capabilities, we'll be able to strike back at Fry in ways we couldn't have dreamed of before. Fry's loss is our gain. It's always been that way.'

'But it's not the same,' barked Slater gruffly. 'Fry threw us away. But he kept *him*, didn't he?' He jabbed an angry finger towards Cameron, still not even sparing him a glance. 'Why do you think that might be?'

Several of the monsters in the audience exchanged concerned looks.

Rora bristled.

'If he was a spy or a saboteur, don't you think he'd have done something to us by now?'

'Yeah – because that's the way spies always work.' Slater shook his head and gave a snort of derision. 'Get a grip, Rora. How do we know Fry didn't *want* us to spring him from the lab? We take him in, and then he takes us down, one by one. He isn't a Reject. He needs to be vetted. Tinker needs to check him over, have a poke around inside and look at his programming. We need to be a hundred per cent sure! A *hundred* per cent!'

There was a loud chorus of assent from several monsters and the room erupted in a rowdy debate. It seemed as if everyone wanted to voice their own opinion but precious few wanted to listen.

Cameron couldn't believe his ears. His new sound filter didn't do anything to shut out ignorance and prejudice. Some of the monsters supporting Slater's rabble-rousing speech looked more human than Cameron did. The idiots were rejecting him as though – what? –

he wasn't a real monster because he wasn't a Reject? Couldn't they see what he looked like? He was more of a mess than them! Whatever this republic was about, the entry require-ments were all twisted and back to front.

He'd heard the saying about how your ears burned when people were talking about you. Now every part of him burned: he was stuck there, forced to listen silently to Slater's snide insinuations.

'Cameron's exactly what we need!' Rora hollered above the din. 'He could be everything we were hoping for. A special weapon in our fight against Fry. Let's not lose sight of that, people!'

He could be *useful*, in other words. In some ways, hearing that was the worst of all. With Rora it was always about what he could do for them, not the other way round. Cameron's blood was boiling. He didn't need this, and he didn't need them.

He slammed his fist down on the table. With a harsh splintering noise, it broke into pieces. A shocked silence fell. Several of the monsters had leaped to their feet, fear in their eyes.

Cameron had their attention now, and he didn't give them time to get over that initial shock.

'I'm not just some weapon! I'm a person! And the fact that none of you seems to get that tells me all I need to know! Who says I want to be part of your stupid republic anyway?'

They were all quiet now, staring at him angrily. Rora shot him a glance that clearly said, *Shut up*. But their anger was nothing compared to his, and Rora's look only fanned the flames. Cameron could feel the heat in what was left of his face.

'So you got me out of that lab. Well, I guess I owe you thanks for that. But that's *all* I owe you! It doesn't mean I have to do what you say. I can look after myself. I've still got friends.'

Cameron turned and stomped off, crunching the remains of the table underfoot. He was at the door when he heard Rora calling his name over a sudden hubbub, and the patter of her light steps running after him. He didn't care. He marched through.

'Hey!' she shouted. 'Even if you're lucky and your friends still recognize you, you'll be putting them in danger as well as yourself! Hey!'

For all he cared, she could shout her throat raw.

Cameron didn't look back.

chapter eleven

a friendly face

As much as he tried to ignore it, Rora's warning still rang in Cameron's ears. And he didn't think that had anything to do with his enhanced hearing. Rather, it was down to the disaster that had unfolded when he tried to contact his family.

This time would be different, he told himself. Firstly, he had to trust that not everything he did would turn into quite such a catastrophe. And secondly, he was determined to be more careful. This time, at least he had use of his in-built phone. What better time to put it to the test? Even if his family was out of bounds, he had other friends back up here in the real world.

Providing some of them had survived the explosion.

Cameron's stomach did a back-flip at the thought. He hadn't considered that. But surely not everyone could have been killed?

Walking along, head down, Cameron paced a little-used back lane behind a row of houses, trying to look as inconspicuous as possible. It was grey and drizzling, with gloomy clouds overhead. The miserable weather was just right for his mood, but more importantly it kept people indoors. At the moment a few wheelie bins and some loose rubbish were all he had for company.

Summoning up the phone function on his HUD, he mentally tapped in Darren's number. He knew it so well he didn't even have to think – he'd dialled the number almost every day since they'd become friends at primary school. He just hoped that it wasn't Darren's mum who picked up the phone . . .

A couple of rings and Darren's voice

answered: 'Hello?'

'Hey, Darren! It's Cameron.'

There was a pause.

'*Cameron?*' Another pause. 'You're having a *laugh*, right?'

'No,' said Cameron. 'Seriously. It's me. As I live and breathe.'

'Live and breathe is right. I mean, God, Cam, they said you were dead.'

'Yeah, well, whatever they said, it's not true. Especially that part. You can tell it's me, right?'

'Yeah, yeah. I mean, I'd know your dulcet tones anywhere. So – what happened?'

Cameron glanced up and down the street. Still no signs of people. 'Well, there was some mix-up with the hospital records. I was, um, badly hurt. But I got out . . . OK.' He couldn't bring himself to say 'in one piece'. He needed to strike a balance between preparing Darren for the truth and not scaring him off. 'To be honest, I look a bit of a mess though.'

'Yeah, me and all,' answered Darren. 'But that's par for the course just after I get up.' He laughed, and Cameron smiled. It was good to hear his friend's usual jokey voice. 'Hey, listen,' continued Darren, 'let's hook up. I wanna hear what happened to you.'

'Yeah, all right,' Cameron replied, relieved that Darren had been the first one to suggest a meeting.

'Cool. Where are you?'

Mentally cursing himself for not having thought of a place in advance, Cameron thought quickly through a handful of options.

'Uh, you remember that building site where we used to skateboard?'

'What, out near the bypass?'

The place Cameron was thinking of was eventually going to be a new shopping centre or something. On Sundays, when there were no workmen around, there had been a whole lot of ramps and obstacles, ideal for stunts. Or for spectacular crashes at any rate. The site itself might be a little too public for what Cameron wanted, but the bypass would offer a bit of cover.

'Yeah, meet me under the flyover there.'

'All right. Give me an hour to make myself presentable.' Darren laughed again, and Cameron laughed with him.

But at the same time he was thinking that he would need a heck of a lot more than an hour to do that himself.

The rain had eased off to a gentle spotting, and the clouds were looking a good deal less threatening by the time Darren came rolling into view on his board.

Cameron waited well under the shelter of the flyover all the same. It wouldn't keep him hidden for long, but he felt like putting off the actual 'unveiling' until the last possible minute. He spent the last few seconds, as Darren scooted up, thinking about what he was going to say. He'd come up with a lot of good-sounding explanations in his head, but he wasn't sure if they would come out right. Or even if he'd get the chance to finish. That all depended on Darren's reaction.

Darren pulled up sharp a few metres off, and flipped the board into his hands with a kick. He looked around uncertainly. He seemed nervous.

Cameron took a deep breath and stepped out of the shadows.

'Hey, Darren.'

For what felt like an hour, Darren stared at Cameron.

'A bit of a mess?' he said finally. 'God. That's the understatement of the century, mate.'

Cameron moved forward, hands raised. Darren took an involuntary step back. His eyes were wide and he swallowed uncomfortably.

'Listen, Darren. Stare all you want. You'll probably need a whole lot of quality staring time to get used to it. And that's fine. I'm still not used to it myself. But I need you to hear me out.'

Darren gave a slow nod. 'OK.'

Carefully, skirting the names and details, Cameron took him through a brief outline of his story. How he'd woken up in the lab and been rescued by a strange girl. How he had discovered what had been done to him, and how he'd come looking for Darren.

His friend listened silently, his eyes widening at certain points, but he didn't butt in and call Cameron a liar or – as was more likely – a nutter. For once, Cameron thought, maybe his new appearance was an advantage, helping to drive the reality home. It was hard to argue with a face like his.

Cameron got to the end of his tale. He paused for a moment, then followed it up with a request. 'Thing is, mate, I need to know more about the accident.'

Darren grimaced. He took a breath, composing himself – probably still fighting his way past the initial shock of seeing Cameron. 'You haven't been following the news, then?'

'No. With everything that's happened, I've been a bit out of touch.'

'You might wish you'd stayed that way.' Darren sniffed. 'It was bad. A huge explosion. They thought they'd have to evacuate the whole town until they realized that it wasn't the reactor that had exploded, so no radiation.

But loads of people were killed. Roger and Alan and Lisa, as well as you . . . and Marie.' Darren bowed his head and shrugged, looking nervous and awkward. 'I'm sorry about that.'

Cameron hadn't mentioned the fact that Marie wasn't exactly dead. For a moment he wondered if he should now tell Darren what had happened to her. But Darren seemed to have taken the rest of the story well. If Cameron went back, he'd have to admit that he'd left stuff out, and he felt sure that would break the trust they were building. Besides, how could he explain it to Darren when he didn't understand it himself? One thing at a time.

'Anyway,' continued Darren, 'they're not sure what caused the accident yet, but the Fry Foundation has been looking after the families of the victims. Arranging counselling, doctors and stuff.'

'Really?' Cameron tried not to sound too sceptical.

'Yeah. Dr Fry has planned this big memorial service next Friday. The whole town's going to be there. The Prime Minister is coming and everything.'

Cameron frowned. 'The Prime Minister's coming here?'

'Yeah, Fry's invited him to give the eulogy.'

'Unreal!' Cameron couldn't believe the hypocrisy. 'It's Dr Fry who made me like this. And it was him who was responsible for that so-called "accident" in the first place.'

Darren looked sideways at Cameron. 'Come off it. What do you mean?'

Cameron braced himself. This was the make or break moment.

'That girl who rescued me, she's part of this . . . community. Fry's been working for the government, creating monsters who are supposed to be brilliant soldiers. And all his Rejects – the ones who managed to get away – have grouped together into something they call the Monster Republic. But that's not important,' he carried on hastily, seeing Darren's brow crease into a frown. 'She was the one who told me all about Fry and his experiments.'

Cameron studied Darren's face as he digested this bombshell. As he expected, Darren shook his head dubiously. 'Come on. Everyone knows that Fry's a good guy. He's been helping the town out for years. Charity stuff and all that.'

'All I know is what I was told. And what I know from the lab.' Cameron gestured again at himself. 'But you have to believe that there's some truth in what I'm saying.'

'Well, there might be something in it,' conceded Darren. 'But you can't trust everything Rora says, can you?'

The penny that dropped right then must have weighed a ton. Cameron had been careful to avoid any specific details like names and places.

So how did Darren know who Rora was?

Cameron covered his surprise and confusion by glancing at his wrist as if he was checking a non-existent watch. 'Well, I reckon I've given you plenty to think about for now, anyway,' he said. 'I'd better be going. Can't hang around too much in daylight with a face like this.' He gave a strained laugh that Darren didn't join in with.

Instead, his friend lowered his head and looked away.

'I'm sorry . . .'

Cameron's heart sank. A swift look to the side told him all he needed to know. Tall, shaggy-shouldered figures had stepped into view from behind the concrete pillars of the flyover.

Bloodhounds.

chapter twelve

carla

'I'm sorry, Cam,' Darren repeated pleadingly as the canine monsters advanced on Cameron. 'They've taken my mum. I didn't have a choice. You'd have done the same, I promise you.'

Cameron grimaced. So Rora had been right again. He'd put his friends in danger. He understood why Darren had betrayed him, but that didn't make it any easier to swallow. A mixture of anger and embarrassment burned in his throat like bile as he choked back a harsh reply, glancing quickly from left to right, calculating his best escape route.

'He's right. He didn't have a choice,' sneered a voice from behind him. Marie's voice, turned ugly. 'So, are you going to come quietly this time, loser?'

Cameron spun round. He could have done without another look into Marie's eyes, now soured with that trademark Carl Monkton hatred. But at the same time, he didn't feel much like standing with his back to her.

'I hope not,' continued Marie. 'Dr Fry still wants you back, but if you ask me, he won't care how many pieces you're in.'

Carl swung Marie's fist at Cameron's face. He should have been ready, but either the monster had learned to move faster, or Cameron was still being fooled by the sight of Marie. Whatever the explanation, he was sent flying.

He landed in the mud, with the Bloodhounds closing in on him.

'Rough him up nice, boys,' the monster laughed, twisting Marie's voice into still more horrible sounds. Cameron leaped to his feet, and braced himself into a combat stance, ready for the Bloodhounds.

Snarling viciously, the canine hybrids came

in at a run, steel jaws snapping. Cameron had to duck or fend off assaults from several directions. He had fought and beaten them before in a blind rage, before he even vaguely understood his new strength and fighting abilities. Now he had a potent new ally – his HUD. The internal display seemed to plot his enemies' attacks, directing Cameron's parries and guiding his own punches to where they would have most impact.

The Bloodhounds were like blunt instruments: dangerous, but direct, with no finesse. They simply tried to grab him and bring him down, or tear at him with their teeth. To Cameron, it was as if they were attacking in slow motion. He could easily outmanoeuvre them, dodging back out of their reach, or ducking in under their blows to deliver devastating counter-punches, more or less at will. It was like pitting a carthorse against a thoroughbred, or a playground bully against a kung fu master.

With a cry, Cameron leaped into the air, evading the jaws of his opponents snapping at his feet, and delivered a well-placed double flying kick that put the last of them down.

He landed and met Marie with an acid grin.

'Looks like your dogs need to go back into training.'

'Looks like I'm needed,' sneered the girl in response. 'But before I go . . .' She grabbed Darren's arm and snapped it like a twig. Darren dropped to his knees, screaming in agony. Marie smiled angelically down at him. 'Just in case you were thinking of chipping in to help your old buddy.'

Cameron stared in horror, immediately regretting his quip about the dogs. This was no joking matter. The brutal violence should have served as final confirmation that the creature he was looking at had nothing of Marie left inside. But as long as his eyes deceived him, it was impossible to accept that as the truth. Focusing on his contempt for Carl rather than his feelings for Marie, Cameron charged and met his enemy halfway.

If the Bloodhounds had turned out to be an easier match this time, this grotesque hybrid of Carl and Marie had, if anything, grown tougher. She evaded Cameron's first kick almost casually, and added injury to insult by trapping his leg and – with a sadistic twist – flipping him onto his back.

'So you beat the Bloodhounds,' said his opponent. 'Big deal. Let's see if you can handle *Carla*.'

Carla? Cameron snapped himself upright, managing to block the next two attacks, but disastrously missing a third. A boot in the face sent him sailing backwards.

'I know you always thought of yourself as a bit of a hero . . .' hissed Carla, leaping closer, ready to continue the assault.

Cameron swept out with a kick, trying to knock her off her feet, but the thing that looked like his girlfriend hopped easily over it and stamped down hard on his leg as she landed.

'. . . but I've got news for you, buddy . . .'

Cameron rolled to his feet, dodging another kick in the process. He spun and whirled with Carla, trading punches in a rapid, brutal succession. She really was quicker than before,

Cameron was sure of it. Maybe Dr Fry had been doing some training of his own. Carl even seemed to have started enjoying being a girl, showing his contempt for Cameron by sneaking little girlish slaps through his defences, before following them up with hard-knuckled rabbit-punches to the jaw or nose.

'. . . you're not meant to be a hero at all . . .'

Cameron doubled over at what felt like a jet-powered kick to the gut. Doing his best to ignore the pain, he switched to defence. Throwing out his arms and legs without thinking, he fought on pure, blind instinct, the way he had first battled the Bloodhounds back at the lab. Still Carla continued to hit home with monster punches and power kicks.

'. . . you're the *villain*. I mean, look at yourself – it's what you were designed for. Why do you think Dr Fry couldn't be bothered to put you together properly? You're disposable! A one-shot wonder! A flash in the pan!'

Cameron growled. He'd had about enough. Actually, he'd had enough ten or twenty blows ago.

'You want flashes?' he snapped. 'How about this?'

He thrust out his right hand to zap his rival with the Taser. Sparks flickered and danced across Carla's body, and Cameron expected to see her flung backwards again.

Instead, she just flashed him one of Marie's smiles and stood there, inviting him to have another go. Turning up the power, Cameron did. Twice. Again the blinding sparks fizzled harmlessly all around Carla's body.

What was wrong? He went to zap her a fourth time, but Carla just blocked his thrust and brought her other arm up for a solid chop to his chest. Then she twisted his mechanical right arm, turning him round, and drove a foot into his back, propelling him into one of the concrete pillars supporting the flyover.

'The thing about working for Dr Fry,' said Carla, marching over towards Cameron's prone body, 'is he's really good about sorting out the little glitches. You tell him you had a problem with electricity, he sorts you out with some insulation. So you keep on improving without even having to try. It's great. Beats the hell out of school.'

Cameron tried to haul himself up, feeling suddenly drained. The last impact had really taken it out of him. With a bleep, his HUD flashed up a message: ENERGY LOW. A level-indicator, like the battery bar on a mobile phone, told the same story, blinking close to empty.

Damn, thought Cameron, shaking his head to try and clear it. He hadn't even considered what power source all his electronic systems used to keep running. Whatever it was, it looked like he'd exhausted it with all those Taser blasts. Something else he had needed to know about his capabilities. Something he'd learned now – too late. His HUD chimed repeatedly: ENERGY LOW.

Cameron translated the bleeps into plainer English: YOU'RE DEAD.

Carla was sauntering towards him, taking her time. She too knew the fight was over.

'Hey!' cried a voice. 'Cameron!'

Scrabbling to pull himself up from the dirt,

Cameron's electronic eye groggily zoomed in on Darren, holding his skateboard aloft with his good arm. He flung it in Cameron's direction. 'Go! Get away!'

Cameron caught the board and, on reflex, dropped it at his feet and stepped on. Carla had reacted as soon as Darren had thrown the skateboard, breaking into a run. She was already coming at him fast. With a last look at Darren, and trying to shut out the insistent bleeping of the alarm in his head, Cameron kicked off. Feeling slightly less battered than the rest of his body, his power-driven legs quickly built up a speed that would have given Rora's motor scooter some competition.

Incredibly, Carla kept on his tail at a flat-out run.

Cameron kicked harder, faster, opening up a gap, metre by precious metre. But a snatched look behind showed that Carla was finding more speed from somewhere too, legs powering unstoppably, pounding the tarmac into submission.

And now she might even be gaining on him,

eating up the space between them as fast as Cameron could feed it to her. It was crazy. Impossible. But it was happening.

Ahead loomed the entrance to the building site. On an impulse, desperate to find some means of shaking off his pursuer, Cameron veered in through the entrance.

He glanced back. No sign of Carla. Had he lost her?

To his left, a loud crash – and a shock. There she was, smashing clean through the wooden fence and coming at Cameron out of a shower of splintered planks. The brute-force short cut closed the distance a bit more.

With shouts of alarm, Cameron saw builders throwing down tools and bricks as they frantically scattered out of his way, swearing at him even as they dived for cover. Then they must have caught a proper look at him – because as their heads came up again, their faces wore stunned, horrified expressions. They stopped swearing and just stared.

Cameron swerved the board to avoid a cement mixer, losing vital seconds. There was a tremendous thump behind him and he knew Carla had just hurdled the obstacle.

'You're mine, Reilly!'

Carla's yell sounded dangerously close. But Cameron couldn't risk looking back to see how close. More obstacles were coming up fast: a JCB, a section of low wall and a pair of enormous metal girders pointing skywards at a steep angle, balanced against a stack of bricks. Lungs burning, Cameron dodged the JCB with scant room to spare, Carla catching up all the while, practically breathing into his ear.

Then a crazy idea lodged in his head. He was never going to outpace Carla on the ground. But what about in the air . . . ?

Desperately Cameron steered for the nearest girder. He kicked and kicked, building up as much raw speed as he could muster. Braced and balanced, there was no time for anything more than the briefest of prayers as he leaned back and nosed the front of the skateboard off the ground.

He hit the girder with a jolt that almost threw him from the board.

But it didn't.

Regaining his balance, Cameron carried on, the skateboard shooting up the length of the narrow iron beam, further and further from the ground. Behind him, Carla shouted again, but Cameron didn't hear the words. He stole the swiftest of glances behind and she was right there, lunging for him. Racing up the narrow girder like an insane tightrope-walker.

Cameron faced front and focused on the end of his impromptu ramp – and the stretch of motorway beyond. He was running out of girder, and this next stunt was going to be *way* trickier than just hitting the ramp had been . . .

As he bent his knees and grabbed the board, he felt Carla's hand snatching at the ends of his hair. Then he was airborne, sailing off the end of the girder – arcing through space, it felt like – clutching the board to his feet.

From somewhere far behind now, it seemed, he heard Carla's scream of frustration. He looked back, and saw her balanced precariously on the tip of the girder, arms windmilling, a furious scowl managing to make her beautiful face ugly. Without the momentum Cameron had gained with the board, she hadn't been able to make the jump.

He had finally shaken off his pursuer.

It was only a small consolation though. Because, as he hit the top of his arc and began accelerating downwards towards the approaching lanes of traffic shooting along in either direction, he realized that the landing was surely going to kill him.

chapter thirteen

running on empty

Soaring through the air, the wind whistling past his face, Cameron clung to the skateboard, desperately trying to coax it towards the gap between lanes. But the motorway was rushing up to meet him too fast. Twisting his body in mid-air, he managed to turn the board enough so that he was at least travelling in the same direction as the traffic. Grazing the top of a huge articulated lorry, he braced himself as he came slamming down on the tarmac just in front of the metal monster.

Cameron felt the board bowing beneath his feet, threatening to snap under the strain but, amazingly, it held. His momentum carrying him forward, Cameron swerved to the left, out of the path of the lorry. The angry driver sounded his horn deafeningly, and Cameron let out an enormous, triumphant 'Whooooo!' in reply, adrenaline surging through him.

But his chance for celebration was short-lived. And he would be too, if he didn't focus right away on dodging the rushing traffic. It didn't help that his HUD was still blinking furiously at him, its supposedly helpful warning now a hazardous distraction as he propelled himself along the narrow corridor between lanes.

Cars and trucks whooshed past, perilously close, swerving violently as they caught sight of him, their after-tow threatening to throw him off balance. Horns blared, drivers and passengers stared with wide eyes, shaking their fists as he whizzed past. Cameron knew that some would soon be on the phone to the police. He had to get off the bypass and out of sight as quickly as possible.

The road ahead curved into a gradually steepening downward slope. As he accelerated downhill, Cameron's first thought was that freewheeling might help him conserve energy. The problem was, the slope didn't show any sign of levelling out and, unlike the cars around him, he didn't have any brakes . . .

The board was racing along now. Cameron had no idea how fast he was going, but he did know that he was testing his reactions – and his nerve – to the limit. He was forced to veer this way and that, dodging cars behind him, in front of him, and rushing past on either side.

Still picking up speed, he weaved past a gleaming Porsche 911, squeezing his board into the gap between it and a high-sided truck thundering the other way. Wind buffeted him from all sides, threatening to knock him under the wheels as he sped through the narrow corridor and shot out the other end.

It was insane. Freakishly insane. Heart pounding, eyes glancing everywhere at once, Cameron looked desperately for a way out of this death-trap.

Finally, ahead of him at the foot of the hill, he spotted a slip road and the sprawl of a service station nestled close to the junction. At once, he was hit by the one thing he wouldn't have objected to being hit by earlier – an idea.

Calculating the distance and the speed of the traffic around him, Cameron's HUD flashed up a pathway through the speeding vehicles and into the slip road. It would be tight, but there didn't seem to be many options.

Bracing himself, Cameron cut across the traffic, aiming for the turnoff.

A protesting squeal of tyres came from behind him, but he'd made it into the slow lane. Breathless, his HUD constantly tracking distance and remapping his trajectory, Cameron steered a tight curve at the base of the hill, veered left into the exit lane and onto the garage forecourt.

He shifted his balance in an attempt to bring the board round in a spinning stop, but he already knew it was hopeless. As if it was punishing him for his speed-freak antics, the board chucked him off and Cameron went clattering and crashing across the tarmac, feeling the hard surface shredding his skin and bashing dents into his metallic parts. He finally slid to a stop against the back wheel of a tatty old flat-bed truck.

Battered and bleeding, Cameron pulled himself back onto his feet. He glanced around for Darren's skateboard, but it was smashed beyond repair.

Time to switch transportation.

The truck was the only vehicle at the pumps. Luckily the driver, a tall burly figure in a hooded top, was inside, paying at the desk. Limping to the back, Cameron hauled himself into the truck, ducked down and pulled a muddy tarpaulin over himself. It was rough and dirty, but Cameron didn't care. For the first time since he'd woken in Fry's lab, he was utterly, genuinely tired. Exhausted, even, as his HUD kept reminding him: ENERGY LOW.

He lay back and closed his good eye. He needed to rest. Just for a moment . . .

* * *

The grumble of the engine jolted Cameron awake in a panic. The truck was moving, and with a shock he realized he had no idea how long it might already have been travelling. He was still groggy and dog-tired and, infuriatingly, his HUD was still blinking away: ENERGY LOW – CRITICAL.

Cameron wished he had some way to shut it off. He tried concentrating on the energy bar and thinking the word 'off', but it just carried on flashing. He stuck another word in front of the 'off', but that didn't work either.

Poking his head out from under the tarpaulin, Cameron saw rows of houses slipping past. The truck was still in Broad Harbour and he thought he recognized the area, but his senses were still too foggy to work out how far he'd come.

Sitting back on the bed of the truck, he let himself get bumped around a bit. If nothing else, the vibration and growl of the engine would keep him awake. Gathering the tarpaulin over his head as a crude sort of hood, Cameron watched the world roll by. The truck seemed to be heading for the outskirts of town, which was a good start. It gave him time to breathe and consider where on earth he was going to go from there.

He shivered, and not just from the cold. The anger and confusion that had been driving him ever since he woke in Fry's laboratory was fading now, replaced by the numbing sensation of fear.

At first, despite the shock of discovering what had been done to him, Cameron had been certain that everything could be put right somehow. Now he wasn't so sure. Everything seemed to be going wrong.

He had walked out on Rora and the Republic. Burned his bridges. Even if he could find his way back, there was no way they would take him in again now. His family had sent him packing – hadn't even recognized him. Now his best friend had betrayed him. Where was there left to turn?

Nowhere. He was on his own. Just the thought made Cameron shiver again. Could he live alone? Make his way somewhere far from civilization, where no one would ever find him?

Impossible! Cameron shook his head. He was too used to being part of a crowd. Hanging out with his friends. Even spending time with his family. He wasn't a loner. He needed company – somewhere he felt he could belong. But where did he belong now?

Slowly an answer slid forward from the shadows at the back of his mind.

What if I do *belong with Dr Fry?*

The idea was insane, of course. Cameron had seen at first hand that Fry was more of a monster than any of his creations. But the thought wouldn't go away. It was lodged in his brain like a sliver of ice.

And was it *really* such a crazy idea? If he did go back to the lab, not only could he get a much-needed recharge but also the training to use all his powers properly. Maybe he could even find out about Marie – if there was some way to undo whatever Fry had done to her . . .

But as much as he was sure Fry could help

him, Cameron was certain that the doctor's help would have a price. And if he put himself at Fry's mercy, what would there be to stop him tweaking Cameron's programming to make sure he was an obedient and unquestioning little soldier? Taking away what little control he had left over his life?

That wasn't a risk he could take. So where did that leave him?

Just then, the sight of a familiar stretch of houses prompted him to sit up. Cameron couldn't believe it: the truck was trundling through his part of town, down a road that ran directly past the end of his street. He sat up, craning his neck for a good look at home.

He half gasped as he caught sight of his mum, his dad and his sister, all of them out by the front gate. Despite the whine of protest from energy-starved motors, Cameron zoomed in on them with his electronic eye. His arm twitched, all set to shoot up and wave.

His heart stopped.

They weren't alone. Men were filing past them, two carting the sofa down the path to an enormous lorry parked against the kerb. As Cameron's truck rumbled on, he caught a glimpse of writing on the side of the lorry, and one word jumped out at him: REMOVALS.

The world hadn't been satisfied with rolling by. The world needed to be cruel. His family were leaving. Leaving home. Leaving town. Leaving him. Apparently they didn't feel there was anything left for them in Broad Harbour either.

Utterly drained, Cameron collapsed back, lying flat on the truck's cargo bed. He didn't much care where it took him now. His HUD flashed pitifully. That zoom must have been the last straw. He could sense his vision dimming, although whether it was from loss of power or the tears that were filling his eye, he couldn't say. He felt his mechanical arm go suddenly dead, becoming a big lead weight at his side. The rumble of the truck's engine grew steadily quieter, as if someone was turning down the volume on the world. His breathing was becoming more laboured and he was vaguely aware of other warning icons flaring feebly up on his HUD, before snuffing out like candles.

As his systems started to shut down one by one, Cameron was way ahead of them, feeling more and more alone. Isolated. In darkness.

Moving was always a nightmare. So much upheaval, so much to organize. And it was a hundred times worse when one of your family was missing. So Rora stayed close to the door, chewing her nails as she supervised the Republic's packing operations, hoping against hope that Cameron would come back through it.

Relocating was a way of life for the Monster Republic, but the fact that it was routine didn't make it any less of a pain. Rora could see the tension she felt reflected in the gazes of everyone who went past, lugging equipment and furniture out of the safe house.

All except Slater. His expression was one of barely concealed satisfaction.

'Expecting someone special?' he asked slyly, lingering over the last word.

'Don't start,' Rora snapped. 'I'm not in the mood.'

'What's got into you, Rora? You going soft? We've never taken non-Rejects into the Republic, you know that.'

'You had your part to play in this,' she accused him flatly. 'You drove him out with just this sort of attitude. Now we're all having to pay for it.'

'Hey, it's not my fault if your new boyfriend happens to be a security risk. But I'm glad you brought it up, because we *will* have to pay if we don't get a shift on. Like, right now. If he's gone back to Fry, the Bloodhounds could be here any minute.'

Rora scowled, and glanced at the doorway again.

'You can go ahead with the others. I'm not budging. If we all move on now, Cameron's not going to be able to find us again.'

'Good point. And he won't be able to lead the Bloodhounds to us, either.'

'Slater, if you don't—'

'If you can't take the tough decisions, Rora,

maybe you should make way for someone who can.'

The room came to a halt. Rora could see that everyone had stopped what they were doing, waiting for the outcome of Slater's blurted challenge.

The moment had finally arrived.

Rora knew how much Slater wanted to lead the Republic, and how long he'd wanted it. But she also knew what sort of a leader he would make. Inflexible. Unsympathetic. He didn't understand that being strong wasn't enough.

Time to put him straight.

She turned to face the taller boy. 'Back off, Slater.'

But he didn't. Instead, he squared up, ready for her. For an instant Rora thought they were going to have to fight it out, there and then, but at that moment a voice echoed through the door.

'I've got him! Cameron. He's hurt!'

Rora's gaze held Slater's for a fraction of a second. They would never know.

The next moment they were both rushing

forward to meet the thick-set monster who was struggling in with an unconscious Cameron hanging off his shoulder.

'Get him to the workshop,' ordered Rora. 'Tinker! Somebody fetch Tinker!'

The assembled monsters jumped into action. Even Slater, she noticed, set off at a run. It was instinct – they were so used to taking Rora's lead that in an emergency they didn't even stop to question. But would it always be that way?

For now she was back in charge, crisis averted. Before long, she was sure, she'd be back to chewing her nails.

chapter fourteen

return of the prodigal

In a brief flash of static, Cameron woke up.

'He'll live,' someone was saying. 'Once the energy r-r-reserves have been r-r-restored, his accelerated healing process will k-k-kick in.'

For one fearful moment Cameron thought he was back in the lab, with the clinical Dr Fry looming over him, delivering his assessment of the 'subject'. But the stammering voice wasn't cold like Fry's, and a quick glance around revealed the faces of Rora, Tinker and Smarts hovering by his bedside. Everyone looked at Cameron as he stirred.

'Hi,' he croaked feebly. 'How'd I get back here?'

'You tell me,' said Rora, pulling up a chair. 'Robbie went out to fill up the truck to move some equipment to a new safe house. When he returned here, he found you in the back. Luckily, we're pretty sure you weren't followed. So how are you feeling?'

Cameron rolled his head experimentally from side to side. 'Stiff neck.'

'Ah, some electrical spillage, I expect. You've got a new power system that we haven't seen before, so Tinker had to plug you into the mains. The current's probably numbed the area around the recharge socket.'

'I have a socket?' Cameron groaned and reached round to the back of his neck. He felt shaken and drained. His battery warning wasn't blinking, though, so he assumed the sensation had more to do with his nerves.

'Leave it alone,' Rora told him, patting his arm. 'Now fill us in on what happened.'

Taking a deep breath, Cameron cast his mind back. The details were still pretty vivid. Slowly he took them all through his meeting with Darren, and the outcome. He tried not to meet Rora's gaze as the subject of Marie reared its ugly head again. 'She's calling herself Carla now. And she was souped up – modified. The Taser didn't work this time.'

Tinker's twitching head nodded even more violently.

'F-F-Fry's like that. Keeps his b-b-best subjects up to date.' He flashed a weak smile at Cameron, eyes downcast.

'Anything else?' asked Smarts gently.

'Darren mentioned that Fry is organizing a memorial service next Friday, for the kids killed in the explosion. The Prime Minister is giving a speech.'

'The Prime Minister . . . ?' Rora frowned. 'That's odd. Why would Fry invite him here when he's trying to close down the Divinity Project?'

'Dunno,' replied Cameron. 'But it's not the only strange thing. Carla said something weird about me being a villain.' He shrugged. 'I don't know why.'

'Can you remember exactly what she said,'

probed Smarts, leaning in. 'It could be important.'

Cameron thought hard. His HUD flickered and suddenly one corner of his vision seemed to change into a TV screen, playing back the encounter.

'I know you always thought of yourself as a bit of a hero, but I've got news for you, buddy – you're not meant to be a hero at all – you're the villain. I mean, look at yourself – it's what you were designed for. Why do you think Dr Fry couldn't be bothered to put you together properly? You're disposable! A one-shot wonder! A flash in the pan!'

Cameron repeated the words precisely.

'I don't know what she meant,' he added. 'But she definitely meant something.'

Smarts gasped. His head tilted sharply to the side, his lips moving in a silent murmur. He appeared to be listening to far-off sounds that no one else could hear.

'Uh-oh. N-n-now you've set him off.' Tinker took a step back, giving Smarts some space.

'What did I do?'

Rora thrust out an arm, stopping Cameron from sitting up. 'He's fine. It's his thing. He takes in so much information that he fills himself up with it. Then he does this – his brain goes into overdrive as he tries to process it all. His mind's looking for patterns, connections, anything he can use to build a clear picture of whatever's going on.'

'Hmm.' Cameron looked warily at Smarts. He couldn't help thinking the kid was having some kind of fit. 'If you're sure it's normal.'

'I never said that,' said Rora with a half-smile. 'But it's normal for Smarts, and that's what matters. You must have given him some important bit of data that his brain latched onto. Now he's got to figure out what it means. We'll just have to wait until he snaps out of it.'

'How long?'

'No more than a couple of hours, usually. Then you can bet he'll have something interesting to say. And fortunately for you, that gives you some time to rest and heal.'

Cameron settled gratefully back on his pillow. He felt exhausted, a bundle of aches and nerves, and he was in no hurry to get up. Besides, whatever Smarts might have to say when he came out of his trance, Cameron wanted to be in top condition, ready for anything.

'T-t-typical,' he heard Tinker saying. 'We finish w-w-waiting for one to w-w-wake up, and now we're w-w-waiting for another!'

Apparently, when Smarts had something to announce, the whole Monster Republic turned up to listen.

Not, thankfully, crowded around Cameron's bedside, though. When Smarts snapped out of his trance, he had quietly requested Rora to call a meeting. An hour later, they were gathering in the common room again. Cameron walked in slowly, just behind Rora. The chairs were arranged in a wide circle, but the setup still reminded him of the previous meeting in the room – the one that had ended with him storming out, smack into trouble.

Well, he made up his mind, that wasn't going to happen a second time. He sat down as soon as he could, taking the weight off his still-shaky legs, and Rora joined him in the next seat. There was Slater, three chairs down. He greeted Cameron with a backward nod and a curl of his lip.

'At least I'm still popular with some people,' murmured Cameron. He hoped Slater stayed quiet. He didn't feel up to toughing it out with him right now.

'Shh.' Rora nudged him.

Smarts stood up. His features were set in an intense frown of concentration, his dark lenses reflecting the faces of the gathering back at them.

'We've made a mistake.'

Smarts let that opening remark sink in for a moment. 'We all assumed that Dr Fry was building Cameron and his other new Divinity Project monsters to use against us, but he isn't. We should have realized this sooner. He doesn't need to destroy the Republic – we're not really a threat to him. We're not the target at all. The target is the Prime Minister.'

A confused mutter rippled around the circle.

'What makes you think that?' demanded Slater.

'On Friday Dr Fry has organized a memorial service for the victims of the power plant explosion. The Prime Minister is delivering the eulogy. I think Fry is going to kill him.'

A stunned silence settled.

'How did you work that out?' asked Rora, her brow furrowed.

'From something Carla let slip to Cameron when they fought last night,' replied Smarts. 'She said that Cameron was meant to be a villain, not a hero. And that he was a one-shot wonder, designed to be disposable. Fry knows that if someone kills the Prime Minister, that person probably won't escape alive – his bodyguards will see to that. It's like playing chess – Fry needs a piece that he can sacrifice. That's what Cameron is.' Smarts paused before delivering the *coup de grâce*. 'He wasn't designed to be a monster-hunter. He was designed to be an assassin.'

Cameron let out an explosive breath. He didn't want to admit it, but Smarts's explanation made a horrible, twisted sort of sense. It certainly explained the gun that was built into his right arm.

'But why does Fry want to kill the Prime Minister?' objected Slater.

'Isn't it obvious?' replied Smarts. 'It's because the Prime Minister is threatening to close down the Divinity Project. We thought that Fry built Cameron in an attempt to try to destroy us, the evidence of his failures, before the government investigators move in. But Fry's more daring than that. It's a gamble, but if he can get rid of the Prime Minister, the investigation won't happen. The Divinity Project will be safe. It wouldn't even surprise me if Fry was hoping to bring the Prime Minister back to life under his control, like he's done with Carla.'

There was a pause, and Cameron could almost hear the other monsters doing their best to digest Smarts's analysis. His own mind was awhirl – Smarts had to be right. The explosion at the power plant had had a double purpose. Not only had it provided Fry with the 'material' for his assassin, it had also created the perfect occasion on which to kill the Prime Minister – the memorial service. As a plan, it bore all the hallmarks of the doctor's trademark ruthless efficiency. It was brilliant, in a sick, clinical way.

But the hard, horrifying truth of it was that yet more cold-blooded murder, in the seemingly benevolent shape of Dr Fry, was coming to Broad Harbour. It was unreal. Horrendous.

So Cameron was surprised by the collective sigh of relief that broke over the group.

Beside him, Rora was watching his puzzled reaction. 'Don't you get it?' she said. 'If Fry's not coming after us, we've got time to leave Broad Harbour! We've been planning to get out sooner or later. Now we might just have time.'

'The mountain base is almost finished,' agreed Slater. 'Even if he does send the Bloodhounds after us, we'll be ready.'

Cameron's mind flashed back to his last glimpse of his family, clearing off with the furniture. They had chosen to run away from Broad Harbour, leaving him behind. Now the Monster Republic was planning the same thing, leaving the Prime Minister and the people of Broad Harbour to their fate.

All his life he'd been popular, but in the last couple of days Cameron had found out what it felt like to be abandoned, and he wouldn't wish it on anybody. Almost without realizing it, he was on his feet, steadying himself for a moment against the back of his chair.

'Wait! So – what? You're just leaving? Running away? You're not going to do anything about the memorial service? We're the only ones who can save the Prime Minister from whatever Fry's cooking up.'

He turned to Rora. To his disgust, she looked as uninterested as the rest.

'So we help him out. And then what?' she demanded. 'Is the Prime Minister going to help us when Fry comes knocking on our door, looking for revenge? Wake up, Cameron. We have to look after ourselves. The Republic is my first priority and it should be yours.'

Slater sneered. 'We'll never be his priority. He's not a Reject. He doesn't believe he's even a monster. He just wants to go home. I've told you, Rora – he doesn't belong here. He never did.'

Cameron gritted his teeth, anger combining with fatigue to make his head swim. These people were infuriating. How long had they all had to come to terms with what they were? Months. Years, some of them. Yet they expected him to do it practically overnight. A dark voice in Cameron's head shouted at him to storm out again, despite everything he'd promised himself.

But this time a note of fear nagged too. He'd already had a taste of how he might manage if he struck out on his own. Battered and alone, how would he fare? If Dr Fry caught up with him a third time, would he be able to fight? He still felt as weak as a kitten after his pummelling from Carla.

Rora thrust her face up towards Cameron's. 'Is Slater right? It's time to choose, Cameron. Our world or theirs. I want you with us – you'd be a huge asset to the Republic – but we can do without you, if we have to. Can you do without us?'

The million-dollar question.

Cameron's feelings were so confused. On the one hand, he was horrified by the callous selfishness of the monsters. Could they seriously ignore a murderous plot against the Prime Minister that could potentially leave the whole of the country to the tender mercies of Dr Fry? It was inhuman.

Then again, what was he, Cameron Reilly? Hardly a Reilly any more – the Reilly family had disowned him. Their Cameron was dead to them, and he hadn't even begun to make up his mind what he was to himself: dead or alive, human or monster?

Where did he fit in the world now? If he was ever going to be a part of the Republic, didn't they have to fit around him as well? Shouldn't it be a two-way deal?

Rora was still staring at him. Everyone waited on his answer.

Cameron hated her for it, but he knew Rora

was right. He couldn't do without the Republic. He had tried going it alone, and look where that had got him – back here, barely able to stand, let alone storm off and make a life for himself on his own.

The bottom line was that he had nowhere else to go, no one else to turn to.

Cameron slumped back into his chair.

Somewhere he heard a voice say, 'OK. Let's go then.'

And after a strange second where he felt detached from everything around him, Cameron recognized the voice as his own.

chapter fifteen

one of the team

The next few days were a blur. There was so much to do that the thoughts weighing heaviest on Cameron had to be set aside. Most of the time, at least. There were still some quieter moments when he sank into gloomy reflection on how devastatingly his life had changed, but he kept such thoughts to himself.

Nobody seemed very interested anyway. His fellow monsters had all been through similar upheavals of their own. Everyone had their losses to bear and their stories to tell, but nobody told them. And when it came to the thing that bothered Cameron most – the clock ticking down to whatever Fry had planned – nobody wanted to know at all. The Monster Republic had turned its back on the town, and Cameron was expected to do the same.

Instead of sharing stories, they shared the workload. The Republic only had two vehicles – the beat-up old truck that had brought Cameron back from the garage, and a slightly larger, slightly less beat-up transit van. That meant many trips to ferry both personnel and essentials out to the new mountain base in an abandoned mine a dozen miles outside Broad Harbour. Cameron was cooped up in the back with a number of his fellow monsters on several trips, working with them on the loading and unloading at either end. And he had to admit that making people work together was a great way of forcing them to talk to one another.

Despite Cameron's reticence and the wariness of most of the Rejects, they slowly got to know each other, bit by awkward bit. There were even a few jokes and a bit of larking about, in an attempt to alleviate the boredom – and the tension.

Smarts and Rora reasoned that, with Fry concentrating on his plot against the Prime Minister, nobody would be following the monsters' movements very closely. Even so, as a precaution, those doing the driving were under orders to take circuitous routes and keep an eye out for anyone trying to tail them. Nobody reported any pursuers, but that didn't stop people watching the roads behind them closely.

Out at the mine, there was plenty to keep everyone occupied and working closely together. There were bunks and other furniture to be installed in the new base, along with a lot of other useful gear and equipment, once they had made the lift operational again. Tinker insisted on bringing his dentist's chair. It was the ideal platform for working on monsters like Cameron whose mechanical enhancements needed repairs and maintenance, and he didn't know where he would find another one like it.

Then there were chains of worklights to rig along all the tunnels and chambers, as well as a water supply that needed to be hooked up. They had to scout out the various ventilation shafts and other exits, and set up motion detectors wired to alarms down in the main caverns. Finally they had to select the best of the mine shafts as their main entrance, ultimately picking one that sloped up at a fairly steep angle to an opening in a hillside, not far from a lonely bend of road.

Through all of it, Cameron was assigned to different work parties, mixing with new teams of people every few days. He sensed Rora's hand behind his shifting schedule, which seemed to change more frequently than anyone else's. He found himself getting introduced to more and more monsters, having to put more names to faces – or half-faces.

He learned that the reptilian-looking monster he'd seen at the first meeting was a girl called Rehana. Originally from Sri Lanka, she'd been a stowaway on a ship that

Dr Fry was using to transport a load of chameleons for use in his experiments. When Rehana was found, Fry had used her in the experiments too.

The monster in the metal visor turned out to be a boy called Alex, another homeless child like Rora. He'd been picked up in one of Fry's regular sweeps through the poorer part of town. The doctor had tried a radical treatment for the skin disease that had caused Alex's parents to abandon him – he had removed his face altogether.

Cameron understood Rora's plan. She was doing what she could to gradually introduce him to all the citizens of the Republic, in the hope that they would grow to accept him. Silently grateful, Cameron played his part, making sure they saw him as a good worker and not a slacker. He put in more hours than he needed to, going the extra mile. Only Slater worked harder, the sour-faced boy seeming determined to out-do him whenever he could.

One afternoon, Cameron was assigned to

work on the shower room with two boys who went by the names of Jace and Freddy. They were a pair of leathery skinned monsters, their bodies twisted and bent out of shape. There was something boar-like about the tusks that poked up over their upper lips, but although they looked fearsome, they had a reputation as a couple of jokers.

They weren't laughing when Cameron's heavy footsteps entered the room, though.

'Hey,' said Cameron, raising his hand in greeting.

'Hey,' they replied, almost too softly to be heard.

Great, thought Cameron. It was going to be one of *those* days.

After they had worked in near-silence for an hour, hauling loose rubble out of the empty chamber and slapping plaster roughly on the crumbling stone walls, they stopped for a break.

Although his enhanced muscles gave him more stamina than a lot of the monsters, several days' hard work had taken their toll, even on Cameron. He sat down, cross-legged, and leaned back against the wall. As he closed his proper eye, he caught a low whisper between Jace and Freddy, who had settled themselves in a corner at the opposite end of the room, about as far away from Cameron as they could get.

'Go on!'

'No way, you ask him!'

Cameron sighed. 'I can hear you anyway, you know, so you might as well talk *to* me.'

Jace and Freddy looked up guiltily, like a pair of schoolboys caught by a teacher they'd been slagging off behind his back.

'What is it you want to know?'

Freddy nervously turned a dusty stone over and over in his hand, the pebble crackling against his hard skin. 'Is it true – that Fry didn't take you from the streets?'

Cameron nodded. 'Yeah.'

'So you had a family, right?' said Jace.

'Right.' Cameron frowned. Where was this going?

'It's just—' began Jace.

'We had a family too,' Freddy blurted. 'Y'know. Before.'

It was difficult to know what to say, so Cameron opted for the obvious. 'What happened?'

'We were kidnapped,' replied Freddy.

'Fry wanted to experiment on twins,' Jace explained, 'but he couldn't wait for homeless twins to just turn up.'

'So we were stolen to order,' said Freddy. 'Someone broke into our room one night. The next thing we know, we're in the lab.'

'Wow,' said Cameron. 'That's a raw deal.'

'You're telling us,' Jace replied.

'Did you try to go back?' Cameron asked. The painful memories of his own failed family reunion were never far from his mind. 'Once you escaped from the lab, I mean.'

Jace nodded. 'We tried, but by then there wasn't anything left. After we were taken, Mum got sick. She died not long after, and Dad moved away.'

'So nothing to go back to,' muttered Freddy bitterly.

'I'm sorry,' said Cameron simply.

'Thanks,' replied Jace. There was a pause. 'A lot of the others, they never really missed their families, because they hardly knew them. The Republic's the only real family they've had. But . . .'

'I think what Jace is trying to say is that we know what it feels like to have your family taken away,' said Freddy. 'And it does get better.'

The leathery twins smiled. At least, Cameron assumed that was what they were doing – their tusks made it hard to tell the difference between a smile and a grimace.

Before he could say anything, Rora entered.

'Hi, guys!'

The trio jumped. Jace and Freddy scuttled back to work.

The fox-girl scanned the room.

'Looking good here. You're at least a day ahead of schedule,' she noted, rewarding Cameron with a pat on the back. 'Good work. You've dedicated yourself to the cause. To the

Republic. You've really become one of the team – I'm proud of you.'

She spoke with a smile that was worth a week's wages to Cameron.

As Rora left, Jace and Freddy turned to each other and grinned.

'What?' said Cameron, but he suspected he already knew what they were getting at.

'Got something going there, eh?'

'With Rora,' snorted Freddy, who had a habit of clarifying whatever Jace said, whether or not it was entirely necessary.

'Yeah,' said Cameron. 'We're real sweethearts.'

Jace and Freddy guffawed as they got back to work, and kept ribbing Cameron all day. But he put up with their teasing gladly. It was just another brand of acceptance.

That night, Cameron stood just inside the main entrance to the base, enjoying the cold air and the feel of the rain on the human parts of his face. The weather looked set to celebrate the completion of the Republic's moving-in operations with a full-blown thunderstorm. Leaving the heavens to do their worst, Cameron retreated down to the newly completed common room for a well-earned meal and an evening of rest and relaxation.

The rough-hewn rock walls didn't exactly make it cosy, but there were plenty of tables and chairs, and even a huge, tattered Persian rug rescued from a tip somewhere. Four monsters were hogging the pool table, but Jace kicked out a chair and invited Cameron to sit and eat with him and Freddy in front of the TV. Apparently a decent movie was due on after the news.

'Cheers,' said Cameron and sat down, keen to get stuck into his dinner. Whoever was on cooking duty had rustled up big platefuls of fish fingers and oven chips, and he was ravenous.

Jace and Freddy chomped messily on their food, chatting between mouthfuls about the day's work and joking about the 'nice atmosphere' here in their new place. Cameron kept half an eye on the screen as the local news bulletin flashed up. Nobody else was at all interested, he noticed. It was as if they had forgotten Broad Harbour as soon as they got outside the city limits.

Shots of flashing blue lights and a burning orange blaze drew Cameron's attention away from the conversation. The sight of the fire engines, the police and the ambulance, and the house belching out smoke and flames, sent an unexpected chill through him.

He knew that house.

'Hey! Someone turn that up!'

Someone obliged by notching up the volume. Everyone in the room turned to watch. The reporter stationed in front of the scene was wearing a particularly sombre expression. Cameron listened with growing shock as the man's words leaped out from the television.

'The dead woman has been named as Angela Harper, a single parent who shared the house with her fourteen-year-old son, who tried to rescue his mother but was beaten back by the flames and has now been taken to hospital. Police suspect foul play and will be conducting a full investigation.'

Cameron stared at the screen, disbelieving.

'Darren,' he muttered in horror. 'They've killed Darren's mum.'

chapter sixteen

taking a stand

The report carried on, but Cameron was no longer listening. Everyone in the room had turned to stare at him. Most of the monsters had heard the story of his escape from Carla, and knew it was Darren who had helped him get away.

Now Darren had paid the price. Cameron felt guilt wash over him like a wave of dirty water. He'd left his friend behind, pretending to himself that he would be OK, even though he knew deep down that he wouldn't.

Cameron looked at the monsters surrounding him, expecting their eyes to accuse him as bitterly as he blamed himself.

But they didn't. In fact, barely anyone would meet his gaze at all. It was almost as if they felt . . . what? Ashamed?

That was it. It was shame in their eyes. The same shame Cameron felt – the shame of doing nothing. Of letting things happen and pretending you couldn't do anything about them. Of taking the easy option, the coward's way out.

That was what Cameron had done by agreeing to the plan to leave Broad Harbour. That's what the rest of the Republic had done by abandoning the town to Dr Fry. What they had all done by trying to make a wrong decision seem right.

As Cameron realized this, he felt something shift within him. Not so much a transformation as something that had been there all along waking up at last. Whatever modifications Dr Fry had inflicted on him, there was plenty inside that hadn't changed. He'd known all along that running away from Broad Harbour was wrong. He'd managed to close his eyes to the fact for a few days, using his fear of being alone to numb his conscience.

But not any more. Cameron knew now that he couldn't live like that, turning his back on the world. And from the look in their eyes, he didn't believe that, deep down, many in the Monster Republic wanted to live like that either. Maybe all they needed was someone to show them that there was another way.

Cameron knew about leading from the front on a football pitch, but this situation was rather different. Or was it? Maybe it was just the same – setting an example and motivating his team-mates. Where to begin? With a team talk, of course. Men of action had to be men of words too. Cameron made up his mind. The circumstances might be strange, but the game was familiar.

Time to give it his best shot.

He started by clearing his throat. 'Listen up,' he said. Then, louder: 'Listen!'

All eyes were suddenly on him. Rora, especially, was regarding him with interest. Someone switched off the TV and he had their full attention. The trick now would be not to waste it.

Cameron gestured at the dead screen, an image of Darren very much in his mind. 'I was responsible for that. I didn't do anything, but I'm responsible just the same. For any of you who don't know, Darren was my best friend.' He allowed the full emotional weight of those words to sink in. 'He helped me escape from Carla when I needed help. Now he's paid the price – his mum was all he had in the world. And where was I when *he* needed *me*? Skulking away in a cave.'

Scattered protests broke out then, but Cameron quickly shut them off.

'I understand it's what the Republic has always had to do to survive. I know that. I'm not having a go at anyone. When you thought that Fry was out to get you, hiding was enough. Staying out of his clutches and finding small ways you could strike back at him. It did the job then.'

A wave of nods passed around the room. Cameron glanced at Rora. Her lips were set in a tight line. It looked as if she'd already worked out where he was going with this . . .

'But now Fry is killing innocent people. He's not just *our* problem – he's everybody's. Most people don't have any way of fighting back. Most of them don't even know he's the enemy. We're Fry's handiwork, and we're the only ones who've got what it takes.'

Cameron walked slowly round to the front of the room, watching the heads turning to follow him. He just hoped he wasn't kidding himself – or, worse, kidding any of the people looking up to him.

'It doesn't matter if the people don't thank us,' he continued. 'It doesn't matter if they fear and hate us. It doesn't matter if they can't understand what we're doing. It's not their words that make us what we are, and it isn't the way any of us look. It's our actions.'

Cameron allowed himself a momentary pause as he reached the front of the room. He took a breath.

Crunch time.

'Someone needs to make a stand, and I can

tell you now, that someone is going to be me. I'm not asking any of you to follow me. I'm just telling you what I'm going to do. This is a free republic, so we all get to choose for ourselves. But, like I said, innocent people are dying. If we stand back and allow that to happen, we *will* be monsters. But if we fight, if we try to defend those people and put a stop to Fry, then we'll be something else. Maybe, in some small way,' he said, with a closing smile, 'we'll be heroes.'

A moment of expectant silence followed, as though the audience weren't sure whether Cameron was finished or not. In the crowd, he caught sight of Tinker's head nodding, although whether in agreement or consternation it was impossible to tell.

The hush wasn't destined to last, however. Initial murmurs quickly gave way to noisy argument and raised voices as people competed to be heard. Cameron grimaced – it wasn't quite the unified effect he'd been aiming for, but he understood that every side had to have its say before they made a decision. Although, as always in these situations, there was always at least one voice who managed to shout down everyone else. And to Cameron's dismay, this time it was Slater's.

'Listen!' roared Slater, stepping out of the crowd a little to Cameron's left. 'We might as well stop arguing! Because let's face it, there are only two sides to this!' He counted them off on his fingers. 'One, we go off on a crusade against Fry and get ourselves killed or – even if we defeat him – get rounded up and stuck in a cage somewhere by the "innocent people" we're supposed to be defending. And for what? We don't even know for certain that Fry had anything to do with this fire.'

'Come off it!' snarled Cameron, thumping his chest. 'Darren was under pressure from Fry's people to sell me out. Darren helps me, and the next thing we know, his mum is dead. It doesn't take a genius to figure it out. Besides, you all know this is the way Fry works.' He pointed at the TV screen. 'You all know exactly what he's capable of. You know that even better than me.'

'All right,' retorted Slater, matching the heat
of Cameron's anger. 'Say Fry is responsible.
So what? We didn't create Fry – he created us.
He's not our responsibility. It's up to the people
out there to wake up to the sort of man he is.
And if we let him carry on the way he's going,
maybe they will. We don't owe them anything.
It's up to us to make a life for ourselves. If we
stick to the way we've been running things,
we can survive and build on everything we've
done so far. That will take time and hard work,
and it means staying hidden. And maybe that's
not *heroic*' – he gave a sneer towards Cameron
– 'but we'd still be doing something worthwhile.
And that does *not* make us monsters.'

Several of the audience looked ready to
break out into quarrelling again, but far more
were holding back, as though they had heard
their own thoughts expressed adequately now
– either by Cameron or Slater. Troublingly for
Cameron, there were quite a number of nods
in the wake of Slater's rousing speech.

Seeing her moment, Rora stepped up to slot
herself in between Cameron and Slater. She

wore a thunderous expression, and Cameron guessed she was either furiously thinking things through or – more likely – just plain furious that the situation was being taken out of her hands.

She raised her arms to quieten those who were still giving vent to their opinions. 'All right. Cameron and Slater have both made their positions quite clear,' she said, flashing them both hard glances. 'But it's not as clear-cut as they seem to think. There are other ways. If we did decide not to intervene now, we'd still carry on the fight, striking back at Fry whenever we can. That's not a cowardly option. We'd still be facing risks every day.' She shot a meaningful look at Cameron. 'There's no question of that.

'*But*,' Rora went on, 'we did take a massive risk to bust Cameron out of the lab. And we did that for a reason – to help us with the fight against Fry. And *maybe*,' she added with a careful measure of reserve, 'we should consider taking that fight to him in a big way. Make a stand, like Cameron says. But whatever we decide, we have to act as one. We're the Monster Republic.' She allowed the name, with its deep significance for everyone in the room, to hang in the air for a moment. 'We can't let this divide us, with one side going off to war and another side staying at home. We all need to be in this together, whichever way we go. It's a big decision, and we need time to think it over.'

'But there is no time!' exploded Cameron. 'The memorial service is tomorrow! We have to decide now, or it will be too late. If Fry manages to kill the Prime Minister and bring him back as a puppet, it will be a hundred times harder to make a stand against them!'

'Cameron—' began Rora through gritted teeth, but he ignored her. The time for talking and thinking was over. It was time for action.

'I think the Republic needs to do this democratically,' he said loudly. 'We need to put it to a vote.'

Nods swelled into a chorus of agreement. Even Slater agreed, looking confident that he would win. Rora glared at Cameron, but he avoided her furious gaze. He knew that with Slater on one side and him on the other, it almost looked like the Monster Republic was electing a new leader. Cameron had no desire to push Rora aside, but he knew she wouldn't see it like that. Well, he'd just have to deal with that later. What mattered right now was the decision.

'Fine,' hissed Rora, turning her back on both Cameron and Slater. 'Have it your way.'

She stepped forward. 'Remember, we're not choosing Cameron's way or Slater's,' she said pointedly. 'We are choosing the Republic's future course. Do we go out there and take the fight to Fry? Or do we focus on making a life for ourselves? All those in favour of taking a stand, raise your hands.'

This was it. Cameron's stomach knotted. Had he said enough? Was he right about these monsters he had only just met? Were they really ready to come out of the shadows? Raising his head high, he thrust his hand into the air.

For a moment the room was full of statues.

Then, slowly, twitchily, Tinker raised his shaking hand to join Cameron's.

It was like a dam breaking. Hands of all shapes, sizes and colours rose into the air. Slater's jaw dropped as he saw the mood change. Rora put forward the other choice and asked the crowd to raise their hands for that, but Cameron's HUD had already tallied the count anyway. There weren't enough monsters left to outvote the others.

He had won.

The Republic was going to war.

chapter seventeen

plan of attack

Things moved fast once the vote was official.

First, Slater stormed out of the room with several of his supporters. Rora only waited long enough to ask Smarts to come up with some sort of plan before she too stalked off, without even looking in Cameron's direction.

So much for the Republic sticking together.

'Don't worry too much,' advised Smarts, appearing almost magically at Cameron's elbow. 'They'll come round.'

'Maybe,' grunted Cameron doubtfully. 'Do you have any ideas for what we should do tomorrow?'

'Meet me back here at five a.m.,' said Smarts.

'I'm going to sleep. I need to think about this.'

'You think in your sleep?'

'Sure,' smiled Smarts. 'Doesn't everyone?'

Cameron watched as Smarts walked slowly out of the room. The blind boy hadn't had enough time to familiarize himself with the layout of the new base, but he refused to use a stick. He was still wearing a large plaster on his forehead from a close encounter with a wall.

The remaining monsters in the room were returning to their regular groups, but Cameron thought he could detect a change in the atmosphere. Several people flashed him a smile, albeit from a safe distance, and he realized that by arguing from within the Republic rather than walking out of it, he had finally won acceptance.

Cameron badly wanted to capitalize on this change. To walk over and join in a conversation and share the mood of quiet but excited optimism. But first things first. He had bridges to mend . . .

* * *

Rora was standing at the top of the mine shaft that led to the surface. She was under cover, but the swirling wind swept rain into her face, plastering auburn fur to her skin.

Cameron came to a stop beside her, with an almost imperceptible hiss of servos. For a long moment there was silence.

'I'm sorry,' he said finally. 'I didn't mean to undermine you as leader.'

Rora didn't move a muscle, her eyes fixed on some lost point in the rainy darkness.

Cameron shifted awkwardly. 'I had to say something. I couldn't pretend any more.'

The fox-girl turned to face him, tilting her head up to look him in the face. There was anger in her eyes, but not the resentful anger Cameron was expecting. Rora's gaze was more frustrated.

'You don't have to explain,' she said. 'I understand why you did it. You might not believe me, but I even agree with you. But you don't know how the Republic works. We're not like a normal part of society – we don't have just one identity. If you knew how much of a struggle it is to hold everyone together, you wouldn't throw ultimatums about so casually.'

'It wasn't an ultimatum,' objected Cameron.

'It was,' growled Rora. 'You turned what should have been a debate into an either/or decision. You didn't leave any room for compromise. What would have happened if you'd lost?'

Cameron was silent. He hadn't really thought that far.

'I'll tell you,' Rora continued. 'You would have gone out on your own and maybe half the Republic would have gone with you. We'd have been divided in two, and both sides would have been easier for Fry to pick off. Brilliant.'

'Do you think that's what Slater's going to do?' asked Cameron.

Rora shrugged. 'Slater loves the Republic. Too much sometimes. I don't think he'll leave.'

She didn't sound very sure, though.

'I'm sorry,' Cameron said again, uselessly.

'Don't be sorry,' replied Rora. 'Just remember that not everyone can afford to be as idealistic as you.'

'Some things are worth fighting for.'

Rora gave Cameron a tired smile. 'I know. But everything has a price too. And we don't know yet what your little speech has cost us.'

A rumble of thunder echoed off the mountainside.

'Are you coming down?' asked Cameron.

'Not yet,' replied Rora. 'I think I need to cool off a bit more.'

'See you tomorrow, then,' said Cameron quietly. 'Sleep well.'

Rora raised an eyebrow. He turned and trudged back down the tunnel. At the first turn, he looked back to see her small figure silhouetted by a bolt of lightning that cut across the sky. And with a flash of inspiration, Cameron realized that she hadn't come up to the surface just to be alone. If Slater was going to leave, he would have to come out this way too. Past her. Rora wasn't cooling off at all – she was on guard duty.

It didn't look as if anyone would be getting much sleep that night.

After a few uneasy hours of dozing, Cameron

returned to the meeting room a few minutes before five a.m. It was cold, but the lights were on and Smarts was already there, sitting in a chair while Tinker hooked up a computer to the TV.

'Slide show,' Smarts said to Cameron, by way of explanation. Cameron had assumed he'd been joking about thinking in his sleep, but the boy-genius certainly sounded perky. If he had been up all night plotting, he looked a lot fresher than Cameron felt. Tinker greeted Cameron with a lopsided grin, which considering he was busy fiddling with connections at the back of the computer, Cameron thought was pretty sociable of him.

Over the next few minutes, more monsters filed in, evidently invited by Smarts. As Rora settled into her usual chair, Cameron tried to catch her eye, wondering what had happened overnight; whether Slater and his supporters had left. But Rora's face was an impassive mask that gave nothing away.

Tinker sat down at the computer. 'We're g-g-good to go.'

'All right,' Smarts began, with a quiet cough to clear his throat. 'Are we sitting comfortably? Then I'll begin.'

As he spoke, the TV screen flashed up a map of the waterfront district of Broad Harbour.

'We're short on time, so I'll keep it brief,' Smarts promised. 'The memorial service is being held on the marina outside the power station – here.'

Tinker tapped the keyboard again and the TV picture switched to an enlarged section of the map. He drew a brisk circle on the computer screen with a stylus, and an area close to the water was suddenly ringed in red.

'It's due to begin in approximately six hours' time. At ten fifty-five a.m. the Prime Minister will go to the podium and unveil the memorial. Some sort of stone obelisk, apparently. Then a two-minute silence will be observed, beginning at ten fifty-eight. Finally, at eleven o'clock, the Prime Minister will begin his speech.'

Smarts panned his dark glasses around the room. 'Now, I calculate that for maximum impact, Fry will strike at the end of the two-minute silence. I reckon that his original plan was for Cameron to shoot the Prime Minister, but since Cameron escaped, that must have changed. Fry knows that this is a suicide mission, and I doubt he's going to risk losing Carla too. We can't be sure what he's got up his sleeve, so Rora and Cameron – suitably disguised – will infiltrate the crowd and see what they can find out. If it turns out that Carla is the assassin, they will try to prevent her from killing the Prime Minister, either subduing her by force or attracting the attention of the police.'

Cameron winced inwardly at the thought of trying to subdue Carla by force. It was easier said than done. Smarts scratched at his cheek as though trying to figure out whether he'd forgotten anything.

'Any questions?'

Everyone's head shook slowly, but nobody spoke.

'Good. Tinker has pulled together some info on the local area. We'll upload it into Cameron and then you can access it whenever you need to.'

As Smarts spoke, Tinker appeared at Cameron's elbow, cable in hand. He bit his lip shyly and nodded towards Cameron's right hand. Cameron grinned, pleased that Tinker had remembered to ask permission this time. He held out his hand and Tinker quickly connected the cable to a port concealed under his thumbnail.

Images and words flashed across his vision at lightning speed as the files uploaded. Again, the new experience was disorientating for Cameron – like being spun around inside a tornado of data. But as the dizziness passed, he saw that dozens of files were now stored in a new folder at the bottom corner of his HUD, ready for access.

The contents looked pretty comprehensive – the whole area mapped out in blueprints, plans and wire-frame images of the power plant and other buildings close to the marina. But Cameron couldn't help wondering how different he would feel when he was actually *there*, so close to the site of the 'accident' that had changed his life for ever.

There was no sense in guessing. The only thing to do now was find out.

As everyone rose to leave, Cameron was surprised to find Slater blocking the door. So he hadn't decided to split off. Yet.

But then what was he doing here? Cameron couldn't believe Slater would want anything to do with whatever Smarts was planning, but he'd clearly been lurking at the back of the room all the time.

'I'm coming along,' Slater declared, levelling a steely gaze at Rora. 'You need someone to watch your back. You can't trust him,' he finished with a jerk of his head towards Cameron.

Cameron swore quietly to himself. Yeah, that made more sense.

'All right,' said Rora.

He stared at her, disbelieving. Then Slater gave him a look, both warning and triumphant – and that was the last straw. Without waiting for Slater or Rora to get out of his way, Cameron barged past and stormed out.

'Hey!' Rora shouted after him.

Cameron didn't stop.

He was getting good at filtering out sounds he had no interest in hearing.

Rora caught up with Cameron while he was locked in a mortal struggle with a dark grey hoodie. Apparently this was the disguise the monsters used on the rare occasions they needed to venture out in the real world. Cameron had the weight advantage, but that didn't make it any easier to get the thing on over his bulky shoulders and generally altered physique without ripping it apart at the seams.

'I'm not in the mood,' he told Rora before she could get a word out.

'I was just going to ask if you wanted a hand with that?'

'I can manage,' growled Cameron, feeling more foolish than ever. He wrestled with the jumper some more and finally managed to yank it down all the way, stretching the material and poking his head up through the neck. He reached behind him to draw the hood up, conscious of Rora still watching him.

'What? If you're waiting for me to say something, then you can forget it.'

He reached for the heavy coat that had been dumped on a chair for him.

'Hey,' Rora said, leaning in front of him and sticking her face where he couldn't avoid seeing her. 'Slater's not coming to protect me. No matter what he says.'

'I know that. He's coming to keep an eye on me. And—'

'Didn't you listen to a thing I said last night?' Rora cut him off angrily. 'There's more at stake here than stopping Fry and saving the Prime Minister. We have to keep the Republic together too. Slater doesn't trust you. Big deal, we all know that. But *I* trust you. And the reason I didn't argue about Slater coming along is that I'm hoping he gets the chance to see you in action. Because if he does, then he'll come to trust you like I do.'

Cameron studied her expression. It was open and honest. Almost despite himself, he found that he believed her. But did that matter? Forget about Rora trusting him – did *he* trust Slater?

He guessed that the answer to that would only be revealed when they reached their destination.

Cameron checked the time on his HUD: 5.57 a.m.

Time to get going.

chapter eighteen

down the drain

At the marina, the memorial service had been organized with all the pomp and circumstance of a state visit. A huge platform had been erected by the waterside for all the civic dignitaries, fronted by a dark wooden podium for the Prime Minister's speech. Facing that was a long spectator stand. Between the two, in the centre of the square, was the new memorial, a tall shape swathed in black silk, waiting to be unveiled. Only the sleek boats moored at the various piers and jetties provided any splashes of colour, but Cameron couldn't imagine any of those wealthy boat owners painting their expensive yachts black just because the occasion was a sad one.

Slater, who had volunteered as getaway driver, steered the van into an available slot in the temporary car park. They were already late. The traffic had been a nightmare coming through Broad Harbour. Most of the town seemed to be on their way to the service. Cameron ground his teeth as precious minutes ticked away.

There wasn't any time to waste.

'Come on,' hissed Rora.

Slater, Cameron and Tinker – all in their hoodies and heavy coats – followed her out of the van and joined the crowd of black suits and dresses making their way towards the spectator stand. Cameron had worried that Tinker's jerky walk might attract unwanted attention, but no one paid much attention to a handful of youths in hoods. Cameron supposed everyone thought Tinker had some kind of unfortunate disability – and nobody looked very close at a kid like that. Or if they did, only out of the corner of their eye, so they could pretend not to be staring.

And if they'd known how Tinker got his 'condition', Cameron wondered, would they have stared then? Would people behave any differently if they knew Tinker wasn't the victim of a disease but of the man Broad Harbour thought of as a saviour?

Cameron didn't expect he'd ever find out. For the twentieth time he reminded himself that today wasn't about making an announcement to the world about Dr Fry. Today was only about saving the Prime Minister. Getting the job done and getting away as quickly and quietly as possible.

It was now 10.23. They had only a matter of minutes before the ceremony was due to start. The four monsters finally reached the spectator stand. It was the obvious place for an assassin to lurk – directly opposite the podium, with a clear line of fire. But the stand was almost full now and a fast scan with his electronic vision told Cameron all he needed to know.

'She's not there,' he muttered to Rora. 'Carla isn't in the stand.'

She cursed, then led the other three

monsters out of sight round the corner of the structure.

'Where else could she be?'

Pulling up the plans of the area that Tinker had uploaded, Cameron zoomed in on all the spots where a sniper could hide. He flicked through the spectrum – normal vision, high-definition, infra-red, ultra-violet.

Nothing.

'Looks like Smarts was right,' muttered Rora. 'Fry's not going to risk Carla being damaged by the Prime Minister's bodyguards.'

'Well, then we're missing something,' grumbled Slater.

'Yeah,' said Rora. 'Like an extra half-hour to search.'

Cameron shut out the bickering voices. He needed to think.

Maybe Carla wasn't going to wait for the Prime Minister openly. Maybe she was hiding away until the crucial moment. But where? Cameron did a 360-degree scan of the marina, on the lookout for inspiration.

His sweeping gaze took in the broad expanse of sea for which the town had been named. Out beyond the cleaner waters of the harbour itself he noticed a few dark streaks on the surface. Patches of flotsam – junk and litter that had clumped together to form temporary landing platforms for the seagulls – were bobbing out to sea, against the tide.

'That's it . . .' he said slowly. With a carefully directed thought-command, he called up another blueprint. The picture flashed up in his mind and appeared as an overlay on his HUD. 'The main clean water outlet drain from the power plant runs right under the marina.'

'So – what does that tell us, exactly?' Rora demanded.

'It tells us we should be looking down there.' Cameron nodded to the manhole cover at his feet. 'We're not the only ones who can hide underground.'

'Of course!' said Rora. 'Fry's not going to run the risk of Carla being discovered. He's keeping her out of sight until it's too late to stop her.'

'So what d-d-do we d-d-do?' gulped Tinker, his tongue working against his front teeth.

Cameron smiled tensely. 'I've spent so much time in sewers lately, I should have realized I'd end up going down a drain again sooner or later.'

Rora laughed quietly as he hoisted off the manhole cover and listened to the rush of water below.

'L-l-looks like the man of the hour's arrived.'

Cameron glanced up and followed Tinker's gaze.

A sleek black limousine was pulling into the square. A small crowd of journalists flocked around the vehicle, hoping to get a snap through the heavily tinted windows.

'Yeah,' said Rora. 'That has to be Fry, all right.'

'How do you know?' asked Cameron.

'Who else would turn up in a more expensive car than the Prime Minister?'

Cameron grimaced. Fry's arrival could only

mean time was running short. But then, he knew that already.

'OK. You guys keep an eye on things up here. I'll take a look down below.'

Slater shook his head, tugging on Rora's arm.

'You aren't seriously going to let him go off on his own, are you?'

'What do you suggest?' she fired back. 'We can't be a hundred per cent certain that Carla is down there. The rest of us have to be ready in case she appears up here.'

'I don't trust him!' growled Slater. 'He could be going to rendezvous with her. They could be in this together!'

'You don't trust Cameron? Well, I do.' Rora's tone was ice-cold. 'And you can either accept that fact, or you can walk away. But whatever you're going to do, do it now.'

Slater's face contorted with fury.

'Have it your way!' He stepped away from the group and vanished into the crowd.

The fox-girl stared implacably after him.

'Rora—' began Cameron.

'Forget it,' she said briskly. 'Some things are worth fighting for, right?'

Cameron nodded.

'So let's fight. Tink and I will take care of things up here. Just – report back soon, OK?'

'Soon as I can,' Cameron assured her.

Rora glanced back at the limo, watching it cross the square at a slow but steady crawl. It had almost reached the guests' platform. 'Now get going.'

Dropping into the hole, Cameron landed thigh-deep in fast-flowing water. Above the roar of the current in the tunnel he heard the scrape of metal as Rora and Tinker slid the cover back into place overhead. The beam of sunshine in which he had been standing, like an actor in a spotlight, disappeared.

Cameron's eye switched to night vision, this time with barely a hint of dizziness. Now, which way to go? He strained his hearing. There was a faint sound further up the drain, in the direction the water was coming from, and his HUD was registering a slow, regular electronic pulse, like a heartbeat.

Carla?

Cameron took a deep breath and trudged off upstream. It would have been tough wading against the current if it hadn't been for his supercharged legs. He smiled ruefully. It was ironic that Fry had given him all these abilities that would, ultimately, make it that little bit easier to defeat him.

Thirty metres along, Cameron spotted a glow. As he cautiously sloshed closer, the light of an LED display stood out brightly in the gloom – flashing in time with the electronic pulse he had been picking up. Maybe it wasn't anything to do with Carla at all.

Confused, he hastened forward into a larger chamber. He could see no sign of Carla. What he could see was the huge stack of plasticine-like bricks set in the middle of the chamber. A tangle of wires connected them to a small round box with an LED display that sat on top of the pile, counting down the seconds. Cameron had seen enough movies to recognize what this combination meant.

The bricks were plastic explosive. The box was a detonator.

It was a bomb.

Cameron looked up at the ceiling. Daylight filtered down, and through the bars of a grating he could see the tip of the silk-wrapped memorial pointing at the sky. The bomb was right under the square, just in front of the Prime Minister's podium.

Cameron felt a wave of fear wash over him, goose pimples crawling across what was left of his skin. He could almost hear the roar of the explosion that had ripped through the power plant. Fry had nearly ended his life completely that day. At the very least he had ended life as Cameron knew it. Now he was trying to do it again to the Prime Minister and countless innocent bystanders.

He crouched down to examine the detonator. The digital display glowed helpfully at him, ticking down the numbers in red. The device was timed to go off at precisely 11 a.m. The end of the two-minute silence.

Smarts was right again.

The sound of splashing footsteps had Cameron on his feet and spinning round.

There, hands on hips and blocking the tunnel behind him, stood the dark and shapely figure of Carla.

'Hello, Reilly. Dr Fry didn't think you'd come. He didn't think you were that stupid. But I told him I knew you better. "This is Reilly we're talking about," I said. "He's stupid enough for anything."'

'This is a bomb, isn't it?' Cameron said.

Carla smirked. 'Did you work that out all by yourself, or did you have help from your freaky Reject friends? Of course it's a bomb. A special present from Dr Fry to the Prime Minister to make sure no one falls asleep in his boring speech. *Boom!*'

'I'm not going to let that happen,' said Cameron firmly.

Carla cracked a grin, clean white teeth gleaming in the gloom.

'I was hoping you were gonna say that.'

She bent into a crouch and stalked towards

him. Cameron circled warily backwards around the bomb, bracing himself against the flow of water against his legs. He raised his fists, ready to fend off the first attack. Ready, he hoped, for anything. Carla followed hungrily, looking for an opportunity to strike.

Then they lunged at each other like two rival lions.

Back above ground, Rora was getting agitated. The fact that they were a man down since Slater had left wasn't helping her mood. Neither was the way Tinker kept looking at his watch between twitches and muttering the time under his breath. Rora could feel the seconds ticking away without a spoken reminder.

All the local dignitaries had taken their seats and there was an air of expectation as Dr Fry went to greet the Prime Minister. The two men were standing slightly apart from the rest of the crowd, far enough for their conversation to be inaudible.

To anyone without fox-tuned hearing.

'Welcome to Broad Harbour, Prime Minister,' said Fry smoothly. 'So glad you could make it to our little memorial service.'

The Prime Minister beamed back at him, making a show of greeting Dr Fry with a friendly pat on the shoulder as they shook hands. But even from a distance Rora could hear that his voice was anything but friendly.

'I couldn't exactly miss it, could I?' he hissed between smiling lips. 'But don't think this means you're off the hook, Fry. I know you're up to something.'

Fry smiled thinly. 'I don't know what you mean, Prime Minister. Please, come this way.'

Now the pair were making their way to the stage, passing along a line of bereaved parents, shaking hands and offering condolences.

Rora was amazed at how a cold-hearted butcher like Fry could pour on the charm.

There was no sign of Carla, but that was a mixed blessing because there was still no sign of Cameron either, and Rora was under no illusions about her own chances in a one-on-one scrap with Fry's monster. Slater would have improved the odds somewhat, but even together they wouldn't have stood much chance. For all his brilliance with machinery, Tinker was next to useless in a fight.

Finally, the Prime Minister shook the last set of hands. He turned towards the VIP stage and extended an arm, inviting Fry to take a seat. Fry shook his silvery head, though, and began walking over to the public spectator stand instead, a humble look on his face.

Rora frowned.

'Why is he going to sit with the plebs?' she muttered, scanning the rows of faces again. There was still no sign of Carla. 'It's as if he doesn't want to be too close to the Prime Minister. He's definitely up to something.' She eyed the unmoving manhole cover. 'What's keeping him?' she hissed.

There was no more time to wonder, though. The Prime Minister had reached his seat, and a black-clad priest was making his way towards the podium to open proceedings.

The ceremony was about to begin.

* * *

Cameron was experiencing a serious case of *déjà vu*.

Once again he was fighting it out with Carla – and once again he was getting the stuffing kicked out of him. The violent splashing of water seemed to be the only difference between this and their last two encounters.

They spun and lashed out with punches and kicks, grabbing each other in wrestling holds. As he fought, Cameron tried to do two things: stay close to the bomb – he was going to need to deal with it fast when the fight was over – and keep repeating the name 'Carla' over and over in his head. He knew that if he was going to win this fight, he would have to forget the girl that used to be Marie. Forget, even, that she'd ever been alive.

It was that heartbreaking thought that lent him an extra burst of rage, and he went at his opponent with a flurry of savage blows, driving her back against the wall. For a moment he had the heartening sense that this time, against the odds, he was going to win. As Carla ducked and dived and tried to sidestep his fists,

Cameron started thinking ahead. Could he disarm the bomb himself or would he have to call Tinker down here?

Taking his mind off the task in hand, though, was not a good idea. Suddenly Carla ducked under his arm, and his right fist crashed into the wall. The mechanical hand sent brick-dust flying. But although he couldn't feel pain in his knuckles, the damage was done elsewhere: Carla came up on his left and drove in with a punch that slammed into the soft part of Cameron's face like a truck into a rabbit.

Cameron spun and toppled backwards, splashing into the water. Dazed, he tried to shake off the blow and get back into the fight. He threw out his arms to lever himself up, but before he could do anything more, Carla was on top of him, sitting on his chest and pinning his arms down with both knees. Cameron writhed and thrashed, but she had him securely held down. Stupidly he opened his mouth to cry out – and water flooded in.

Carla planted a hand over Cameron's face and pushed his head down under the surface of the water. He tried for a kick, but she was too far up on his chest. Thrashing wildly, he glimpsed Marie's blurred face through the slosh and swirl of water. She was smiling down at him, but it was a cruel, laughing smile as she watched his vain struggles. Cameron felt a burning pain growing in his chest as his lungs cried out for air, and he tried to fight harder, but by now his heavy coat was completely waterlogged and pulling him down.

As Carla continued to laugh at him from above, the sight of her through the churning water grew murkier and more distant, and Cameron realized with a sick feeling that he was finished. There was nothing more he could do to fight, and he was going to drown.

chapter nineteen

zero hour

To a round of subdued applause, the Prime Minister tugged on a black velvet cord and unveiled the memorial. It was a simple black marble obelisk, a plaque affixed to one side with the names of the deceased children etched in brass. No one could read it from where they sat, of course, but they didn't have to. As the Prime Minister made his way to the podium, the priest solemnly listed the names of the dead.

'... Marie Lyons, Carl Monkton ... Cameron Reilly ...'

The irony of the list didn't escape Rora – especially that Marie and Carl came next to each other in alphabetical order. She and

Tinker had moved closer to the spectator stand in case Carla should make a sudden appearance there, but had picked a spot where they could still keep an eye on the drain where they had seen Cameron disappear.

'Four minutes to eleven,' said Tinker, so nervous he seemed to have forgotten his stammer.

'It's been too long,' replied Rora. 'Carla must be down there. I'm going to help.'

As she spoke, the manhole cover moved. The sigh of relief was halfway out of her when her heart froze solid in her chest.

Instead of Cameron, the athletic figure of Carla was hoisting herself easily out from the drain. Quietly replacing the manhole cover, she stole a surreptitious glance around. As the monster's gaze swung towards them, Rora and Smarts turned away and tried to look inconspicuous.

'D-d-did she see us?' breathed Tinker.

'I don't know,' replied Rora, slowly raising her head.

Carla had vanished.

'Damn!' Rora's head snapped round. 'Where did she go?'

'I c-c-can't see her,' said Tinker.

'If Smarts is right, she's going to make her move at the end of the two-minute silence. That means we've got four minutes to find her. Maybe we can cause a panic, a distraction, anything.'

Tinker's jerking head nodded. 'What about C-C-Cameron?'

Rora swallowed hard. As much as she didn't want to believe it, there was nothing else she could say.

'If he was down there with Carla, he's dead.'

Cameron floated in a world of green. The burning pain in his chest had been replaced by a hollow, leaden ache that seemed to get more distant by the second. Everything was very peaceful, his mind drifting like his body.

Suddenly a penetrating chime sounded in his head and flashing words burst across his vision: BACKUP OXYGEN SYSTEM ACTIVATED.

Instantly Cameron's mind seemed to snap back into gear. There was an overwhelming taste of salt in his mouth. He was still under water! His arms thrashed about in immediate, reflexive panic.

It took him a moment to realize that there was air in his lungs. He wasn't exactly breathing under water, but oxygen was being pumped into him from somewhere. He stopped struggling and tried to calm himself. It looked as if he had another thing to thank Dr Fry for. Although, he reminded himself, if it wasn't for Fry, he wouldn't have been in this mess in the first place.

One look was enough to tell Cameron he wasn't inside the outlet pipe any more. Daylight gleamed down through the water above him. He kicked upwards and swam towards it.

Cameron popped his head above the surface and spat out sea water, before drawing in a deep breath and taking a swift glance around.

The marina was behind him. He was out in the harbour. After he had stopped struggling,

Carla must have left him for dead, to be washed down the pipe and out to sea. He hadn't drifted far, though. He could still make out the crowds of people gathered on the marina. There were no screams, no sounds of panic. It looked like the bomb hadn't gone off yet. There was still time.

Checking his HUD to see that the breathing system was still operating, Cameron ducked quickly back below the surface. With powerful strokes, he swam back towards land, his eyes searching around for the pipe outlet.

As he swam, he wondered why Carla hadn't thought about the emergency oxygen system. Surely she must have been fitted with a similar device? Arrogance – and ignorance – had to be the answer. Even in his own body, Carl had had more than enough of both before the modifications. Now that he was rendered superhuman, the arrogance would only have got worse. Enough to blind him to such little details.

Cameron had to be thankful for small mercies.

What he was more thankful for, though, was the cold, hard lesson he had learned. Finally he knew beyond all doubt that the monster he was facing was Carl. Nothing to do with Marie at all. Her body was only a shell, the disguise or costume in which Dr Fry had dressed his champion. Her body had probably been chosen for the Divinity Project because she was fit and strong. But Marie would never have delighted in violence the way Carl had – he'd always enjoyed inflicting pain and shoving people around. And so Fry had selected Carl's brain for its brutal, thuggish mentality. The combination had made for a formidable soldier. Marie could never have been that.

Kicking strongly through the water, Cameron made a promise to himself never to make the mistake of confusing the two again. It was time to take on Carl – Carla – and her alone. And although he knew now that he couldn't be drowned, Cameron had realized something else too. He was never going to be able to beat Carla in a fair fight. He was going to have to out-think his enemy.

But first there was the small matter of defusing a bomb.

Reaching the outlet, Cameron pulled himself into the pipe, battling against the flow. Soon he was able to stand, breaking the surface to race back along the pipe to where the bomb was still ticking down to zero hour.

Cameron swallowed as he saw the timer: 10.58.

He had been out of the picture far too long.

Frantically he set to work on the detonator as the seconds bled away.

Rora shoved her way through the crowd, panic rising in her chest. There was no time – and no sign of Carla. But she was here somewhere. Getting ready to strike.

On the podium, the Prime Minister spoke.

'And now I ask you to join me in two minutes' silence to remember the children who lost their lives in this terrible tragedy.'

Silence fell like a shroud. Hands were joined, heads bowed, lips moved in soundless prayer. With Tinker at her side, Rora strained her eyes and ears for any trace of movement or noise.

Nothing.

She sought out Dr Fry in the spectator stand, hoping against hope that Carla would be with him.

There she was! At his right hand, just where a loyal bodyguard should be. Beside her, Fry sat stock-still, his hard, bright eyes never straying from the Prime Minister. Then he smiled. A cold, heartless smile that turned Rora's blood to ice.

It was about to happen.

Desperately Rora started to barge forward, elbowing her way towards them, but she knew she was too far away. Tinker snatched at her sleeve.

'D-d-don't, Rora! We're too late.'

At the same instant a tall figure leaped out of the crowd towards Fry. Rora caught sight of a flash of dark hair and sharp features.

'Slater!' she screamed.

In the distance, the town hall clock could be heard chiming the first strike of eleven. Time seemed to slow to a crawl. Rora could see everything unfolding in slow motion.

Carla unwinding from her seat to intercept Slater before he could reach Fry . . .

The Prime Minister peering over at the disturbance with obvious confusion . . .

Fry's gaze sliding away from the wrestling monsters next to him and back to the podium, excited expectation still written across his face . . .

The clock chimed again and again.

Slater and Carla grappling, the girl forcing Slater down to his knees . . .

Fry rising to his feet, his hands gripping the back of the seat in front of him . . .

The clock chimed one last time. The eleventh hour had come.

And Fry's face changed.

The triumphant smile was wiped away. And in its place was frowning confusion and thinly concealed frustration.

Carla struck Slater a blow that sent him sprawling to the ground. She pointed her arm directly into his face. Even from a distance

Rora could see the gun barrel protruding from her wrist.

The world snapped back into real time.

'Time to die, Reject,' snarled Carla.

Rora raced forward, but there was no way she could reach them in time.

She didn't have to.

Dust and cobblestones exploded into the centre of the square as Cameron erupted through the ground. He was streaked with filth and bare-chested, and with his various mechanical extras in plain view, he looked like some hideous creature from the bowels of the earth.

'Time's up, Dr Fry!' he announced as he landed, crouched and ready for action.

The stunned crowd stood aghast. Too shocked even to move.

Slamming Slater's head into the ground, Carla stepped forward into the square.

'You just can't stay dead, can you, Reilly?'

'It's the way I'm made. Here, take a closer look.'

Cameron swung his fist, and Carla threw out a blocking arm, smiling.

'Let's dance.'

The two monsters spun across the square, Carla giving a two-for-one deal on kicks and punches. It was only to be expected: she was Fry's champion; Cameron was one of his Rejects. She was faster, quicker, stronger. She had every advantage.

And this time round, that was what Cameron was counting on.

Carla's grin spread millimetre by millimetre as her attacks slammed into him. For once, she was silent as she fought, doing all her talking with her fists. Cameron fell back towards the centre of the square, drawing Carla away from the crowds, who still remained motionless and dumb, staring in disbelief at the fight – and the monsters who were battling it out.

A flurry of punches sent Cameron staggering backwards. Almost losing his footing, he quickly bent his knees and turned the tumble into a spring, somersaulting through the air onto the top of the marble memorial obelisk.

With the grace of a panther, Carla leaped up

to join him, treating him to a spinning kick as she landed. Nearly toppling backwards off the memorial, he crouched to steady himself – and that cost him heavily. Standing over him, Carla pounded Cameron with a rain of punches. No style, no finesse, just pure brute force hammering down on his head and shoulders.

He could feel every blow beating down, noisily bashing dents in the metal sections of his upper body and threatening to cave in his reinforced skull. There was no break, no let-up in the punishment, and it was all he could do to get his mechanical arm up to shield himself from the onslaught.

The move bought Cameron a split-second to look around. The Prime Minister had vanished beneath a scrum of bodyguards, who were dragging him off the podium towards safety. The crowd had finally recovered their senses, and were backing away towards the edges of the square. The only people any closer were a few photographers, holding their cameras high and snapping off picture after picture.

It was time.

Before the next punch could fall, Cameron slipped a small object out of his pocket. Then he sprang up from his crouch with every scrap of strength left in his motor-driven legs. He sailed clear over Carla's head, spinning in mid-air, to land halfway across the square, facing his opponent. The crowd fell back further, muttering fearfully. Cameron ignored them.

Carla turned to face him, curling her lip in a sneer.

'Fancy aerobatics won't save you, Reilly.'

Cameron stared back, taking one last look at Marie's gorgeous face.

'Talking of aerobatics,' he said, 'reckon you can fly, Monkton?'

He nodded at Carla's feet. She glanced down.

There, on top of the obelisk, was a small round box, trailing wires. An LED clock display had stopped at the time the box had been severed from its power supply: 10:59:53.

The detonator.

Cameron clicked the mechanical fingers of his right hand and Carla's dumbfounded expression disappeared in a ball of flame.

chapter twenty

in memoriam

Pandemonium erupted.

The crowd had seen enough. More than enough. The occasion wasn't about remembering the dead any more: it was about fleeing for their lives. As a billowing cloud of dust filled the air, people ran everywhere at once, in a panic to get away from the explosion and the monsters that had caused it. Police officers already struggling to move in were now met head-on by a stampede in the opposite direction.

On the other side of the square, through the flying grit, Cameron could just see Rora and Tinker helping Slater to his feet. They had thrown off their disguises and their terrifying appearance was keeping the chaotic crowd at bay. Rora waved to Cameron, pointing towards the place where the van was parked. He was about to run over to join them when he saw a familiar figure slipping round the side of the spectator stand in the other direction.

Dr Fry was heading for his black limousine, clearly hoping to get away unseen in the confusion. Cameron broke into a run, ducking and weaving past the milling people – or barging them aside where he had to. Launching himself into a final high-jump, he spun in the air and landed expertly between Fry and his car.

'Hello, Cameron.' Lazarus Fry had the gall to look at his watch. 'I'm afraid I don't have time to stop and chat. But if there's anything you need to discuss, feel free to call my secretary for an appointment.'

Cameron glared, advancing a step towards the doctor, poised to spring in either direction if he decided to make a break for it. Fry didn't move, though. He eyed Cameron coldly.

'You may have thrown us out with the garbage,' Cameron said, 'but we've scrapped your precious plans, good and proper.'

He didn't know what reaction he was expecting from Fry. Anger? Frustration? Fear? But he certainly wasn't expecting the doctor to throw back his head and laugh.

'I don't remember enhancing your ability to kid yourself. But maybe I should have concentrated on building up your brainpower as well as your muscles.' Fry gestured around at the chaos. 'Take a good look, Cameron. You and your friends have done a far better job at sowing terror and panic than I could ever have managed with a bullet or a bomb. I can already see the headlines in the papers tomorrow: MONSTERS RUN AMOK AT MEMORIAL SERVICE. Gosh, with headlines like that, I shouldn't be surprised if we make the national news. TV crews will be flooding here to try and capture one of the Broad Harbour monsters on camera. How long do you think the good citizens of this country will support a prime minister who allows all these disasters to happen? He'll be out of Downing Street before the end of the month – thanks to you and your ragtag band of Rejects.'

Cameron scowled murderously. 'Maybe you're right. But no matter what happens after this, at least nobody else has to die.' He threw out a hand and clamped his fingers around Fry's throat. 'Except you.'

Fry didn't move a muscle. Even with Cameron's hands at his neck, he maintained an infuriating air of superiority, his nostrils flaring as he eyed Cameron contemptuously.

'There's still Marie,' he croaked, forcing the words up through his constricted throat. 'I could bring her back.'

Involuntarily, Cameron's grip weakened.

His mind slipped back to that moment when he was drowning: through the swirling water all he could see was Marie's blurred face. Only this time, he was recalling her smiles, the real her.

'I have her brain stored safely,' whispered Fry. 'In a secret and highly secure location, of course.'

The words wormed their way beneath Cameron's skin. He had said his final goodbyes to Marie. Now Fry was taunting him with the possibility of seeing her again. But how could that ever be? The detonator had destroyed her body completely. Surely not even Fry could patch her together again?

'Yes,' continued Fry, as if he was reading Cameron's thoughts, 'I could bring her back. Even in a body very much like the one she used to have. And I could show you the true extent of your powers too, Cameron. Show you what you really are. There's really no end to the miracles I can perform.' He smiled tightly. He could see that Cameron had taken his bait. The hook had worked its way in to stay.

'I could do all this. *If* you came over to my side, that is. But if you kill me, you'll never see her again. Is that what you want? Think quickly, Cameron – we have company.'

Out of the corner of his eye, Cameron glimpsed several police officers heading towards them. He gritted his teeth. He wanted nothing more than to apply the final pressure that would squeeze the life out of his enemy, his tormentor. But the thought of Marie refused to go away. It was as if she was standing beside him, whispering in his ear, holding him back. His fingers slipped from Fry's neck.

'I can see you need more time to think about it,' said the doctor reasonably, adjusting his tie. 'Well, when you're ready to know what you really are, you can come and find me.'

'I know who I am now,' Cameron retorted. 'But if you try to hurt any of my friends again, I will come and find you. And you'll wish I hadn't.'

Lazarus Fry favoured Cameron with a parting smile. 'We'll see.'

Then he turned and walked briskly to his car. As the limousine pulled away, footsteps rushed up to Cameron. He turned, expecting to find a policeman. Instead, he was greeted by the sight of a young photographer shoving a camera towards him. Cameron threw up a hand, his boosted reflexes making sure he had shielded his face before the flash went off.

Still, better not leave anything to chance. Snaking out his right arm, he snatched the camera from the guy and crumpled it in one hand like a Coke can. Pieces fell between his fingers and dropped to the ground.

The photographer looked on, stunned, as Cameron turned and loped away. On the other side of the car park, the Republic's old van was waiting, engine running. Inside, Cameron could see Rora and Tinker holding the doors open for him.

'Wait!' called the photographer. 'Who are you?'

Cameron didn't look back.

'I'm a monster.'

THERE, BURNED AND TATTERED, LAY A HUMAN ARM - WITH NO BODY ATTACHED.

THE FIGURES SEEMED TO BE SOME HIDEOUS HYBRID
OF MAN, MACHINE AND ANIMAL.

HE SHOULD HAVE EXPECTED IT BUT THE SIGHT WAS STILL A SHOCK.

WITH A DULL CLANK, THE DOOR OPENED...

SHE WAS SMALLER THAN HE
HAD REALIZED, TINY AND
LITHE, WITH DARK,
ELFIN FEATURES.